"Can't we stop soon?" Arien moaned. "We've been running all night."

Berrian lifted his head. "Soon. I smell a river in the north wind. If there is a river near, it will be the great river of Fellheath, the Fellflood, which flows from the mountains to the Great Forest. When we cross the Fellflood, we'll enter the high reaches of Vivrandon. There we'll be safe; the warriors won't cross the river."

"Why not?"

"That part of Vivrandon is more wild than Fellheath. Goblins live there, it is said; the only men who survive there are sorcerers or outlaws."

"*That's* where we're going to be safe?"

A MagicQuest Book

The Hawks of Fellheath

PAUL R. FISHER

TEMPO BOOKS, NEW YORK

THE HAWKS OF FELLHEATH

A Tempo Book/published by arrangement with
Atheneum

PRINTING HISTORY
Atheneum edition/1980
Tempo edition/June 1984

ISBN: 0-441-31906-8

Tempo Books are published by The Berkley Publishing Group,
200 Madison Avenue, New York, New York 10016.
Tempo Books are registered in the United States Patent Office.
PRINTED IN THE UNITED STATES OF AMERICA

To Scott, from both of us

Of Garren's daughters, Amreth shall claim three,
One of valley, one of fell, and one of tree;
One queen of light, one queen of flood, one queen of briar,
One sought by love, one taught by scorn, one wrought by fire.

One shall lift her husband's sun
With magic from an aeddenon.

One shall fell enchantment find
The gates of Vivrandon to bind.

But Fellflood's angry oath shall break
For a wilted blossom's sake.

And when wars and warlocks all are gone
Will Amreth's daughters seek the dawn.

Contents

SAGA THREE

SAGA FOUR

SAGA THREE

• 1 •
Council Eve

FROM all around Moleander there rose the smell of apples.

The taste of apples stained his fingertips and lips, and the fragrance of apples made his nose tingle. The aroma of apples clung to his tunic and nested in his hair; it collected around him like smoke. But he ignored it, concentrating instead on an apple above him. It quivered on a branch just beyond his reach. Bracing himself he stretched, pushing upward until his hand slid along the bough to just inches from where the apple hung. But his fingers snatched only leaves, and he knew he couldn't reach the apple without losing his balance. He glanced at his half-filled pail, then at a basket propped near it, which was heaped with apples.

"Fflad!" he called to the boy on the branch below him. Fflad, an apple in each hand and one in the crook of his arm, looked up. "Fflad. I wish you'd tell me something."

"Anything you like." Fflad dropped the apples into his basket.

"I haven't half filled one pail, and you're finishing your second basket. How do you pick so fast?"

Fflad shrugged and reached for another apple. "Quick

3

fingers," he replied. "A bonus from years of practicing the harp." His eyes flickered up toward Moleander. "It also helps," he added, "if you find a thick clump of apples and pick among them so you don't have to reach so much. Reaching takes time."

Moleander shot a glance at the apple above, and nodded. "If you ever decide not to be a minstrel, you'd make a good farmer."

Fflad laughed. "Come on, Mole. You know I'll never be good for much but ballads and music. To tell you the truth, I don't like picking apples. I hate picking apples, in fact. I have to play games with myself to keep working—"

"At least you work," Mole put in. He nodded toward the base of the tree, where two boys were tossing apple cores at one another. "Orne and Llan have picked about two apples each all afternoon. And every apple they pick, they eat."

"Or throw," Fflad said as he watched a bit of apple soar into a nearby tree.

"They're too young for orchard duty," Mole said. "I don't blame them for throwing cores. The rest of us, though," Mole glared in the direction of Gareth, sitting nearby, "ought to be working."

Astride a limb near the ground, Gareth lay back against the tree. Until that moment he had been munching on an apple, holding a near-empty basket between his knees. He raised his dark head toward Mole. "I've done one basketful already, Mole, so don't look at me like that. And don't say *you* enjoy this any more than I do, because I know you don't." He smiled tartly. "I'd give anything to be out of this tree and back at the Tutory. I want to be ready when I meet with the masters tonight. This apple picking is so dull!"

"Nobody likes to help with the harvest," Mole answered, "but it's the least we can do in return for King Ellarwy's kindness. After all, he feeds us, and we'll be eating these apples this winter."

"True, I suppose," Gareth said. "But I could be so much more useful elsewhere. I'm not an apple picker; I'm a loremaster. If I were in any other realm, I'd be loremaster to the king. I ought to be writing chronicles or studying ancient records, not climbing around in apple trees!''

Mole lowered his eyebrows. He looked first at Fflad, then at Gareth. "Is a loremaster better than a minstrel?" he said. "Or do you think a loremaster is better than the King of Thrinedor?''

After a moment, Gareth's eyes fell. "I suppose not. But I don't see *you* picking many apples, Moleander Ammarbane!''

For answer Mole snatched an apple near his foot and flung it into his bucket. It rang dully against the iron of the pail.

As Mole climbed to a higher branch, Fflad slipped from the limb beneath to pour his load into a great wooden box between the rows of trees. He vanished behind a screen of leaves as Mole worked his way upward.

The greatest concentration of apples, it seemed, was near the top of the tree, though the fruit everywhere was sparse. Even patches that appeared thick from below seemed scattered when he climbed in among them. So Mole was high in the tree before he wedged his pail on a forked branch and propped himself to work.

There, in the topmost branches, Mole could see the breeze sifting the layered leaves below; he could sense the tree trembling with his weight; it was almost as if he could feel his own tug against the tree's roots, as if he could feel the frailness of its hold in the earth. Yet the movement of the tree was not unpleasant, and it gave Mole a sense of grandeur to sit so high.

For one thing, the view was breathtaking. He could gaze out over the breeze-bent crests of all the other trees. Green and laced with afternoon shadow, the orchard was spread below him in an odd combination of pattern and chaos. The apple orchard ended at a pear orchard in the east, the half-hidden stripe of the river in the west, and the dusty cart track on the north, where a wagon moved, loaded with several apple bins. The trees themselves were a sea of movement; the ripple of wind-combed leaves, the flash of bright clothes beneath the boughs, and the sunny murmur of conversation along the rows. From somewhere down in his own tree, Mole heard Llan's voice raised in an indignant shout.

When he had come halfway down the tree again, Mole realized that he had added only three apples to his load. But the view had been too interesting to do more. Besides, the laughter and talk from below seemed more important.

When he reached the center of the tree, he found the others gathered on the largest limb. With the exception of Fflad, they all ate apples and swung their legs in the space below. As Mole arrived, Fflad, surrounded by grins and apple baskets, was speaking.

"And, of course, I had started back along the beach toward the village, and I didn't think to look back until I had reached the first pier. It was then, of course, that Llan caught up with me and told me that Orne had fallen into the sea and was covered with seaweed."

Chuckling followed, mostly from Llan.

"Reminiscing about Eber Seador?"

Startled, Fflad looked up. Then he nodded. "You must admit," he said, "we had a lovely time at Eber Seador. At least I did. The sea begets good poetry, as Cyranus said. Do you remember the white beaches, the grass growing up to the edge of the sand from the hills? Do you remember the breakers foaming, making those funny little tracings in the sand? Do you remember the great grey rocks like ghost ships straddling the tides? I was amazed how far the sea stretched; it seemed forever—"

"Bother the sea," Llan interrupted. He swatted at a fly on his apple. "It won't do us any good to wish for it when we can't have it. And it's so hot! I wasn't built for heat. I hate this late summer weather. I wish we were at Seador now. Or on Mon Ceth, where I could jump into a snowdrift!"

Although Mole had thought the day pleasantly warm, he began to feel that his collar was too tight when he saw Llan's flushed face.

Orne, meanwhile, had climbed up and sat down on the bough next to Mole. "I hope we get to go to Eber Seador again next summer," he said. "It was lots of fun falling in the sea, even though the seaweed was kind of sticky."

Mole laughed. "I'm sure it was. But I doubt that Master Dafydd will try to take the whole academy to the coast again, not after Owan and his friends went sailing in that fishing boat without asking." Mole looked down into the orchard. "Next summer let's plan our own adventure, without the rest of Avy-Ellarwch. I for one would like to see Mon Ceth again.''

"It would be nice to see Misty Mountain again," Fflad said. "And by now it may be a rather pleasant place to visit. I'm sure there are fewer goblins and wolfmen there. Not to mention less snow.''

"It's settled, then," Mole said. "We'll go back next summer. Perhaps we can even go in the spring, if Arien can get away—'' Mole stopped short and stared blankly at Orne. "Arien," he repeated. "Where is Arien, anyway?''

Fflad looked at the apples in his lap. "I haven't seen her since breakfast. In fact, I'm not even sure I saw her then.''

"Well, she must be in the orchard someplace," Mole said. He craned his neck to look between the trees. "I know the girls from Avy-Ellarwch are here; I saw that red-headed friend of Arien's, that Enna, a few minutes ago. But if she's her , why haven't we seen her? She knows we always weed the same row and pick from the same tree.''

"She might not have come from the castle with the other girls," Fflad suggested. "You know how busy she gets at the Tutory sometimes.''

Mole didn't answer. Instead he leaped to the ground, his pail cradled against his chest. "If she's coming," he said simply, "she'll be here soon." He strode through the weeds toward the bin. "If she isn't, she must be busy someplace else. In the meantime we'd better do a bit of the work we were sent here to do." Mole frowned toward Llan. "This time I want everybody to work. *Everybody*. And anybody who throws an apple," he added with a menacing grin, "can have an apple fight with me.''

When he saw that the others had gone to work, Mole emptied his pail of apples into the crate, kneeling to watch the russet skins of the apples as they tumbled over one another. He lingered a moment after the pail was empty, twisting a stalk of grass. The warmth of the sun on his face woke a number of thoughts, ideas that he turned and tasted in his mind. He had scarcely set his pail among the weeds, however, when he heard hoofbeats.

Hooves pounded between the trees. Mole, looking up, saw

a blur of white against the green of the orchard. It took him only a moment to realize the patch of white was a horse in canter; it took him only a moment more to recognize the stallion and its blond, green-clad rider. No one in Thrinedor had a steed so white. And no one else in Thrinedor wore a tunic of Thrinedor green belted with silver links. It could only be Berrian, son of King Ellarwy, the crown prince of the kingdom.

Berrian noticed Mole at a healthy distance and reined his horse to a halt with a neat sidestep. Gleaming trappings blinded Mole, but when the prince wheeled his horse toward the tree, Mole saw that Berrian was not alone in the saddle.

"Arien!" Mole shouted.

Arien tossed her hair back. "Hello, Mole." She turned toward the tree. "Hello, everybody."

"Hello, apple pickers," Prince Berrian called out. He collected the reins easily in one hand, then helped Arien from the saddle with his free arm. He smiled at her. "Here we are, Lady Arien."

Arien curtsied slightly. "Thank you very much for the ride," she said. "It would have been a long walk without your kindness. I would never have reached the orchard before sunset at the rate I was going."

Berrian cocked an eyebrow. "It was my pleasure."

Lifting the pail, Mole moved nearer. "It was very generous of the Prince of Thrinedor to offer you a ride," Mole said, pushing the words to the tip of his tongue. "But if you had come on the cart from Avy-Ellarwch with the other girls, you wouldn't have been obliged to walk, either."

"If," Arien said. "But it wasn't that simple. I had a . . . a project to finish at the Tutory before I came. So I couldn't ride on the cart." She nodded to Berrian. "It was very good of Prince Berrian to bring me here, especially when it was so out of his way. He is supposed to meet the Lords of Northmarch at the Ford of Thrine."

Mole forced a smile. "It was good of the prince to do you the favor," he said in a low voice, "with everything else he has to do. So you're meeting dignitaries for tomorrow night's council, eh?"

"Indeed." Prince Berrian straightened the circlet he wore as a crown. "It is therefore with great regret that I must leave you to your apple picking—"

"Feel free to stay and work with us if you like."

With hands on the reins, Berrian beamed blandly. "I would love to, Moleander, but I simply don't have the time."

"Your father has the time."

"My father! All my father thinks of are his fields and orchards. If the preparation for the council were left up to him, there'd still be laundry hanging from the battlements and straw stacked in the great hall." Berrian looked at Mole with cool blue eyes. "I don't have the time my father does to hoe beets and weed corn. I have the reputation of Thrinedor to keep up." Prince Berrian turned his horse away, then peered over his shoulder as an afterthought. "One more thing, Moleander. Have you been invited to the council? I can't seem to remember."

"I was invited," Mole answered between clenched teeth. "Were you?"

To this Prince Berrian only laughed. Then with a last smile at Arien, he spurred his horse into a trot. In a moment the stallion disappeared into the trees. The tinkling of silver trappings faded back into the murmur of the orchard.

"Was I invited, indeed." Mole sniffed.

He felt a touch at his elbow and looked over to meet Arien's eyes. "You're not upset, are you?"

"Upset? Why should I be upset?"

Arien shrugged. "You look a bit red, that's all, a bit red in the cheeks. I'd forgotten that you and Prince Berrian sometimes have . . . disagreements, when I accepted his offer—"

Llan interrupted. "Yes. Mole doesn't like Berrian, not since Berrian beat him in that sword match at the summer games—"

"He didn't beat me." Mole took the pail under his arm. "It was a draw, for neither of us scored a hit. They declared him the winner only because the judge was one of Berrian's royal cousins from the coast!"

Arien, however, did not seem to be listening. She turned toward the tree to answer a question from Fflad. "I did ask

Berrian about Gwarthan,'' she said. ''He told me that Gwarthan was invited to the council; but that doesn't mean he'll come, as you and I both know. Wizards are difficult people to plan on. Especially small wizards.''

''Arien!'' Llan shouted from a high branch, where he and Orne now sat poking at one another. ''How come you got lucky enough to ride on Prince Berrian's horse? He never gives *me* a ride. If I had a horse like that, I'd give rides to every boy who asked for one.''

''If you had a horse like that,'' Orne countered, ''you'd be a handsome prince like Berrian and wouldn't want to give anybody rides.''

Mole gripped his bucket and moved around the tree, away from the others. He began to jerk fruit from the lower branches; in a matter of minutes he had filled his pail. Yet he did not immediately take his load to the bin; instead he turned to look past the trees.

Perched on a green hill, Ranath Thrine, the royal seat of Thrinedor, thrust up above the sun-soaked leaves. The castle's nearest wall was dotted with windows and darkened with russet shadow. Its three towers scratched against a large grey cloud that rose from the moorlands in the north. The castle and the lower buildings of the school, Avy-Ellarwch, built against its right wall, were a familiar sight. But now, by some effect of shadow, the fortress seemed imposing. Black stripes from the watchtowers fell across the gate, and its tawny stone seemed almost crimson.

Then Mole spied a bird circling against the northern clouds. It had to be a large bird, a hawk or eagle, for though it was far off, the beat of its wings was clearly visible. It was odd, Mole thought, that a hawk should come here, so far from the mountains; it might have been one of King Ellarwy's falcons except that no other birds were in the sky to hunt. Mole followed the bird's flight until it disappeared beyond the castle hill. As the bird disappeared, he fancied he heard the echo of its scream in the breeze. In spite of the sunlight on his arms, Mole shivered.

A branch snapped behind him, followed by a yelp, an explosion of leaves, and the thump of something striking the ground. Mole let his apples fall to the grass and dashed back around the tree.

He met the others leaping from the limbs. Out of the corner of his eye he saw Orne, pale-faced, scrambling down from a high branch. Gareth, Fflad, and Arien had clumped around Llan, who lay against a confusion of high grass and fallen apple twigs.

Mole shoved Gareth aside and knelt beside Llan. The boy's green tunic was torn near the shoulder, disclosing a broad scrape whose lines quickly filled with blood. Llan's eyes were closed, his face was the color of the undersides of the apple leaves, and his body hung limp in Arien's arms.

Mole looked at Fflad.

"He fell," Fflad explained, biting his lip. "He and Orne were on that branch up there, and he lost his balance—"

"He didn't lose his balance," Orne said from behind. "He didn't. I pushed him. I didn't mean to, but I did. We were just knocking at each other for fun, like we always do. I didn't mean to push him off the branch. I didn't. Mole! Is he all right?"

Before Mole could speak, Llan began to wheeze and then to cough. He groaned faintly, then winced when his eyes met the sun. "Ouch," he muttered. "Did I fall from the tree?"

Mole nodded.

"Remind me not to do it again. Is Orne here?"

"I'm here," Orne piped, wedging in between Mole and Fflad. "Are you all right, Llan? I'm sorry I made you fall!"

"It's my fault as much as it's yours," Llan returned. "Don't worry about it, Orne—ouch!"

"Here," Mole said. "Let me help you up."

With Fflad's help Mole began to lift Llan from the ground. But Llan had scarcely cleared the fallen leaves when he cried out. His body stiffened, and he threw his head back against the earth. For moments after Mole and Fflad set him back down, he panted and looked from face to face, wild-eyed. "I can't get up! Not just yet, anyway." He blinked back tears as Mole gingerly examined the bruise on his shoulder. When Llan's eyes touched Orne's, he sighed. "Don't look so glum," he told Orne with a frown. "I'll be able to get up in a moment. I just need a bit of rest before I get on my feet again. Then I'll race you back to the cart!"

●   ●   ●

Cold moonlight stole through the window that night and crept across the floor to where Moleander sat at a table in the room he shared with his friends. A candle burned at his left, casting an oval of light over an open book and on an uneven scrawl of ink atop an age-curled sheet of parchment.

Mole put down the quill he held and bounced to his feet. He wriggled and scratched to rid himself of stiffness. A puff of the night breeze drew him toward the window, and before he knew what he was doing, he leaned over the sill into the darkness.

Cool night had fallen on Thrinedor. The two pole stars, Orygath and Penegir, gleamed in the north, jewellike. The whole sky over the thatched roofs of Avy-Ellarwch was peppered with stars. From somewhere beneath the battlements of Ranath Thrine, the River Thrine rumbled in its bed; nearer and softer, the fountain in the courtyard pool bubbled. The night breeze whispered in the mountain ash, the great tree of Avy-Ellarwch. A few lights winked from the girls' housings. Still more lights, hidden by the tree, glinted from the Tutory, the long hall of Avy-Ellarwch where Gareth was meeting with the masters and where Llan slept in their care.

A voice, above the plucked runs of a harp, interrupted Mole's thoughts. "You don't need to worry about Llan," Fflad said. "The masters will care for him well enough."

"Well enough," Mole agreed. "But the question is whether well enough is good enough. I ought to visit Llan and see if there's anything I can do for him."

Fflad, in the shadows near his bed, put his lyre aside. "You can visit him tomorrow, when you won't disturb his sleep. In the meantime he'll be all right; the healing master told me that he was only jolted by his fall. He ought to be back here with us in a few days."

With a restless bounce in his step, Mole returned to his seat. His gaze wandered to the two mattresses by the fireplace and the one boy tangled in his woolen blanket. Orne's face, framed by a mane of straw-colored hair, looked pallid in the moonlight. "This place seems empty without Llan," he said. His arms suddenly were cold. "I almost miss him and Orne whispering until midnight. And it's harder on Orne than it is on me."

Fflad nodded. "He thinks it's all his fault. He must have apologized to Llan fifty times in the cart from the orchard to the castle."

"I only wish the council weren't tomorrow. Otherwise I could stay with Llan and have a good talk with Orne. As it is, I'll have to be at Ranath Thrine all day tomorrow—"

"Come now, my boy," said a voice from the wall. "Don't deceive yourself. You don't *have* to be at Ranath Thrine all day tomorrow. You simply *want to*. You're afraid you might miss some of that silly lot of princes and warriors."

Mole's eyes rose to the stone wall above the table, to Sodrith, the Sword of Speech, hanging between two iron bolts. The sapphires on the Sword's hilt sparkled.

"That isn't true! At least not entirely. King Ellarwy asked me to help ready the Upper Hall for the assembly."

"That, I suppose, takes all day," said the Sword. "Though I wouldn't be surprised where you're concerned."

"Bother you," Mole snapped. He snatched up the parchment on the table, strode to Fflad's bed, and deposited it in Fflad's lap.

Fflad cocked an eyebrow quizzically. "The Kings of Thrinedor? I thought we memorized that genealogy last summer—"

"We did. Most of us," Mole returned uncomfortably. "I didn't think it was worth the bother before, but with the council coming up tomorrow evening, I thought I'd . . . er . . . brush up. Test me, will you?"

"How many Kings of Thrinedor have there been?"

"Four," Mole answered.

"Five," Fflad corrected. "That is, five if you count King Ellarwy."

Mole frowned. "I did count King Ellarwy. And I know there were four." He raised a finger. "Hwyl the Good, Thrinenil, Ellarwch, the king who founded this academy, the Ellarwy. That's four."

"You forgot King Llarandil," Fflad said. "Although he was a High King of the Kingdoms, he is considered to be the first king of Thrinedor, too."

"But Thrinedor hadn't been founded in Llarandil's time!"
Fflad threw up his hands. "I didn't make up history—"

"I'm sorry. Ask another question."

"All right. Who will be the next king of Thrinedor?"

Although Mole heard Fflad's question perfectly, he cupped a hand to his ear.

"Who is the Crown Prince of Thrinedor?" Fflad repeated.

Instead of answering Mole moved to the window. "I haven't the faintest," he said. "I give up."

"Come on, Mole. I hope you're not still angry about this afternoon. You mustn't blame Prince Berrian simply because he had the courtesy to bring Arien to the apple orchard. You must remember that each of us is a guest of Prince Berrian's father. King Ellarwy might just as well have turned us away when we came here after you killed Ammar. He didn't have to feed, educate, and care for us. But he did. And he has been caring for us for two years."

Mole didn't reply. He had no grudge against King Ellarwy.

Over the roof of the girls' lodgings, the lights of the village peeped among the hills. Against the glow of the rising moon Mole could make out the dim outline of the Mon Dau in the east; he followed their black zigzag southward until his eyes met the frame of the window. But his imagination continued on, following the night-hidden range farther south, to the place near the river where a mountain, wreathed in grey mist, waited. Even in the soft breeze of the Thrinedor autumn, Mole could smell on the edge of his memory pine and storms and snow. He could almost hear the tap of snowflakes against thorns, the bellows of distant night things beyond the mist. Suddenly his hands curled around the edge of the window, and an excitement like the call of a war horn sounded within him. The corners of his mouth tightened as he whirled around.

"I've been so uneasy lately," he said to Fflad. "And now I think I know why."

Fflad looked up from tuning his lyre. "Why?"

"Because I need an adventure. Fflad, what you said about King Ellarwy's hospitality is true—we've been here two years, almost. That's too long to presume on his kindness. And that's all the learning and the apple picking and feasting I can take. Do you realize how long it's been since we've had an adventure?"

"Yes," Fflad returned crisply. "Two months. Since we went to Seador."

Mole frowned. "I mean a *real* adventure."

"All right. If you don't count that, two years." Fflad winced a little at a sour note from his lyre, then looked up at Mole. "But I think it's been rather pleasant these two years. Living here at Avy-Ellarwch is easier on the nerves than living on Misty Mountain was. Mole, you get plenty of sword fighting and such, and I'm free to read Cyranus and compose songs. To tell you the truth," Fflad added, "I don't miss cold, frightening adventures in the least."

"I'm not talking about cold, frightening adventures. I'm talking about brisk, comfortable ones. Sleeping beneath the stars, listening to the mutterings of the north wind, rushing along narrow mountain heaths. Doesn't that sound as enchanting as any of your ballads?"

"If you're in the mood for enchanters," Fflad broke in, stretching a string, "you'll have your fill of them at the council. Rumor has it that Gwarthan will be there. And even if he isn't, you'll be discussing that sorcerer, the Black Counselor of Vivrandon, who has risen in Fellheath. In fact, if the council proposes action against Vivrandon, you may well fill your taste for adventure with war."

Though Fflad's expression was grim, Mole beamed. But he sobered when he glimpsed, out of the corner of his eye, the long staff of ash wood bracketed beneath the Sword. "I hope it won't be war," he said. "But the council will break this monotony in one way or another."

All the same, Fflad had teased Mole's imagination, and before he knew what he was doing, he was at the window again. He looked at the ebony rises of Fellheath in the darkness far north of the river. He could sense something waiting there, something smelling faintly of iron and musty feathers; he fancied he saw a fleet shape arch against the stars.

His thoughts of sorcerers and vast lands, however, drained from his mind when he saw the Tutory door open. It spilled a sphere of yellow light onto the blue courtyard and with it a boy, who, once the door had closed, started toward the boys' quarters.

"It's Gareth," Mole whispered to Fflad.

A moment later soft footfalls approached in the corridor outside the room. The door swung open. Gareth, dark eyes glinting, stepped into the candlelight, a broad grin on his face.

"Hello, Mole. Fflad. I'm back. I'm sorry I took so long. But this wasn't my usual interview with the masters. In fact, it turned out not to be with the masters at all, although Master Dafydd was there most of the time."

Mole saw that Fflad had paled. "If you didn't meet with the masters," he asked, "then who *did* you meet with?"

Grinning more broadly than ever, Gareth clapped his hands together.

"Not so loud," Mole cautioned. "You'll wake Orne."

"I hope I wake him." Gareth chuckled. "He ought to hear the news, too."

"What news?"

Gareth looked from Mole to Fflad, then back to Mole again. "I met with two underlords from Sharicom who came here for the council," he said. "They were polite, cool and confident. I like that. If the other lords of Sharicom are the same, I shall enjoy Sharicom very much."

"Sharicom?"

"Sharicom. I've been offered a post as a loremaster there. I'm to become a custodian of King Cashma's own library, as an assistant to one of the greatest chroniclers in the Kingdoms. I'm to be given food and shelter for my services and a chair next to King Cashma himself."

Mole did not reply.

Fflad rose to his feet. "That certainly is a noble offer, one well worth considering." Fflad glanced sidelong at Mole. "Did you . . . accept?"

Gareth's eyes widened. "Did I accept, Fflad? Did I accept. What do you take me for, a fool? Of course, I accepted. I said yes in an instant. Offers like that don't come along every day." He paused. "Why are both of you looking at me like that? You look as if I'd done something wrong—"

"You haven't done anything wrong," Mole said, "but you might have given yourself a bit of time to think this whole thing out. There are so many considerations! The rest of us, for instance."

Blank, Gareth pondered before answering. "You'll all receive posts, sooner or later, if that's what you mean. You as a swordsman, and Fflad as a minstrel—"

"I could have harped for the King of Crywyll," Fflad said. "I was offered gold to go to Crywyll last spring. But I didn't choose to go. I chose to stay here instead."

"So that's it," Gareth stormed, "that's it! You're so noble, Fflad, giving up a good post to stay here in Thrinedor with our old group from Mon Ceth. But you made your choice. And your choice isn't mine."

"I've always thought of us," Mole said with a grimace, "as more than just friends. That's why I went to such trouble to see that we boys all got the same room here at Avy-Ellarwch and that Arien was housed nearby. We are much more than friends, Gareth. We're in fact like family."

Gareth sighed and turned toward the window. "But even families break up," he said quietly. "If you were my father and Fflad my brother, my decision would still be the same. Don't you see? This is my chance, Mole. This is my chance to go out on my own, to depend on my own wits and means. This is my way to get out of apple picking and bean weeding and shield practicing. I'll be able to do what I love, keep records and study genealogies." He spun around and faced Mole. "It's not what the two of you are making of it. I'm not leaving you forever or anything like that. Sharicom's not as far off as you seem to think. I'll come back to visit. Maybe more often than you'll like!"

Mole lifted his eyes.

"Don't argue with me," Gareth warned. "I've made up my mind."

"When are you to leave for Sharicom?" Fflad asked.

"When the underlords return after the council."

Mole dreamed of rain.

He dreamed it was autumn. The rain pattered on the roof. Occasionally he felt a drop splash across his cheek. Beyond the window the storm wind driving the rain against the walls of Avy-Ellarwch almost made a song, a chant without melody. The rolling of thunder-drums in the high hills of Thrinedor formed a beat of words, but Mole dared not listen to them; he clasped his hands over his ears to shut them out.

Then the dream changed and darkness closed over him like a blanket.

The moon, like a silver ship, rose on a tide of cloud. Here and there in the heavens twinkled the lighthouses of the stars. Again the wind sang, but the melody was softer. It was a song as beautiful and sad as it was old, full of the smell of mist, the sound of water dripping in caverns, and the sight through trees of a rider on a white horse.

·2·

The War Horns of Thrinedor

A THRUSH chirped in a mountain ash as Mole emerged from the boys' quarters. Cold mist hung canopylike over the courtyard and lifted over the chimneys of the Tutory. The square was empty and silent, for the children of Avy-Ellarwch still slept; only the fountain beneath the tree gurgled to break the dawn numbness.

Mole belted the Sword on his hips and started toward the door of the Tutory. He had gone only a few steps, however, before he noted his hands, which even in the faint morning light were noticeably smudged with dirt. He touched his face only to realize that it was probably in a similar state; or if it hadn't been, it was now. He remembered how Arien had always needled him about his grubby appearance when they were children. If he was going to see her then, it would be wise to be a bit more prepared.

After checking for faces in the windows around the courtyard, he went to the fountain and knelt on the flagstones at its edge. Morning was hardly the time to do one's washing; Mole could feel the chill lifting from the glassy surface of the pool. Minutes passed before he finally plunged his hands in.

The water was still and glossy, like quicksilver. It reflected a face topped with a storm of soot-colored hair, a face whose dark eyebrows were drawn together in puzzlement. Mole watched the face adjust its green collar and dip its hands into the water. The face blurred and rippled as he splashed the water on his cheeks and neck, but it reappeared when he wiped his hands on his flanks.

He brought a picture of Prince Berrian to his mind as he stood up. He compared it with the now-distant face in the pond. Lingering in indecision, he stood between the two visions, examining each critically. But soon the faces faded, his own before the other, and shaking the last droplets from his fingers he started off toward the Tutory doors.

He had scarcely raised his head, however, when he realized that his activity at the fountain had been observed. A girl perched on the steps beside the tree shaking a worn rug into the morning breeze watched Mole with keen eyes.

"Good morning," she said, grinning. Her hair, the color of oak leaves in autumn, curled thickly around her head in the shape, Mole decided, of a dandelion gone to seed.

Mole brushed his damp bangs aside. "Morning, Enna."

Although he had been shivering, he now felt oddly warm under Enna's stare. "If you're looking for Arien," she said, batting the rug against her legs, "you won't find her in the scullery."

"She's asleep, then?"

Enna shook her head. "Arien?" She laughed. "No. She was up hours ago."

"Then she'll be in the kitchens. That's her work—"

"That *was* her work," Enna corrected. "It was until last night, when she was released from all her tasks at the Tutory."

"By whom?" Mole demanded.

Enna pouted carelessly. "How should I know? Do I know everything? The only thing I know is that when Arien came in last night, she told me that she wouldn't have to work in the Tutory anymore."

"She didn't tell me."

"Arien is close-mouthed about things nowadays," Enna continued, draping the rug over one arm, "so I didn't try to get the details. In fact, I'm not even sure there *are* any details, at least none that Arien knows. But I have my own personal suspicion that Arien's good fortune comes from someone in Ranath Thrine.''

Mole felt that he must be turning red. But he asked, dreading the answer, "Then where has she gone this morning?"

"What am I, Arien's mother? I just sleep in the same room with her, and not much more; she doesn't confide in me, though I don't know why. But since you want my opinion, I'll tell you that I think she's gone to the same place she's been going for the last month. Lately she's been even more secretive than usual, sneaking out early in the morning and creeping in late at night. She's been talking in her sleep about it, but Arien is simply impossible to understand when she sleep talks."

"Never mind that. I need to find her. Enna, I've got something important to tell her. Do you have any idea where she is?"

Enna raised an eyebrow. "Something important to tell her?"

"Very important."

Enna blinked, expectantly.

Mole frowned. "It's just that I've got to tell her that Gareth is leaving for Sharicom tomorrow . . ."

"Gareth?" questioned Enna blankly. "Gareth. Oh yes, the little one who is always dropping leaves down girls' backs."

"No," Mole said stiffly. "Gareth's the one who studied to be a loremaster."

"Oh. I'm sorry. I do seem to get Arien's friends mixed up."

"You were going to tell me where Arien has gone."

"I'd tell you if I knew," Enna said, turning back toward the door. "But the fact is that I don't have the foggiest idea. For all I know, Arien could be goblin-hunting in the Mon Dau." She looked over her shoulder as she started back into the girls' housing. "But if you should happen to come up with Arien, do come back and tell me where she was. If she's flirting with Master Dafydd, I want to know about it."

With this Enna left Mole standing alone in the courtyard.

"If you asked me," the voice of the Sword said, "it's not hard to figure out where your Arien has gone—"

"I don't recall," Mole retorted huskily, "having asked you at all."

Once Mole left the gate of Avy-Ellarwch, the sun lifted far

enough above the Mon Dau to reveal the details of the land, so Mole paused long enough to look and to stomach the indignation that came from his encounter with Enna.

The land shone green and gold as far as the eye could reach. From the heights of the hill upon which both Ranath Thrine and Avy-Ellarwch had been built, Mole could see most of western Thrinedor and a good portion of Pesten as well.

Westward the fields of Thrinedor glimmered: emerald squares of corn and orchards marching toward Eber Seador and the sea. Here and there patches of woodland broke the lines of the fields, and byres poked among the trees along yellow meadows threaded by silver brooks.

Northwestward lay a small farming village tucked in the hills. Dimly behind rose the pale line that marked the edge of the high moors of Vivrandon, called Fellheath, below which hung the perpetual vapors of the Thrinefens, the source of the Thrine. The skies over the moors seemed to be clear that morning except for a watery streak of cloud, shaped oddly like a bird in flight, poised above the cliffs.

Shaking back the sudden memory of a dream, Mole started down the path toward the fortress gate. The packed-earth path presently met a broad lane climbing the hill from the fords on the Thrine. Here Mole paused again to survey the trees along the river, in search, perhaps, of a flicker of white in the green.

His search was interrupted, however, by a party of strong men garbed in work clothes who trotted merrily down the lane from the castle gate. At their head strode a substantial man with tawny beard and hair, who was stuffed in a tunic obviously too small for him. In one hand he wielded a stout hoe and in the other an immense burlap sack.

"Good morning, Your Majesty," Mole said as the men approached.

"It certainly is," King Ellarwy replied. He beamed broadly and paused to shake hands with Mole. "Are you ready for the council, Moleander?"

"Almost."

The king turned a moon-shaped face to his men. "We're ready—almost—as well. Actually we thought we were ready—completely—until my good wife began to supervise the victuals for after the council. We're short on vegetables, so I and my lords are off to bring back a bag of beans."

"It's easier on the back to be a peasant," one of the Lords said.

Laughter rumbled among the nobles, most heavily from King Ellarwy. "If we want to eat it, we have to pick it. There'll be time for being noble and such at the feast tonight, although"—a shadow shifted on King Ellarwy's face—"although none of us may be in the mood to eat."

Gloom spread to the faces of the other lords.

"Speaking of the council," Mole said hastily, "I'll need to begin setting up the tables soon. I'd like a bit of help, if you could manage to get me some, sire." Mole paused. "Is Prince Berrian around this morning?"

The king looked thoughtful. "No. I don't think he is. He often goes riding this time of the morning, you know. But come to think of it, I believe he went to Avy-Ellarwch on an errand for his mother—I seem to recall something of that nature being said during the talk about the vegetables. But if you want help, you shall have it. My other sons are loitering around the courtyard."

"Thank you, sire," Mole said listlessly.

As the king and his lords left, Mole could not help but think how little King Ellarwy reminded him of High King Gion. Not only in appearance, but in mannerism, though Ellarwy did not strike Mole as being less of a king than Gion. Ellarwy was cheerful; Gion was solemn. Ellarwy gave the impression of the outdoors, of rain and orchards, ale and horses. Gion brought to mind things quiet and ancient, things noble and dusty and sundrenched. Suddenly Mole wanted to see Gion again; he wished the High King were coming to the council, although he knew no such visit was expected.

"Gion," Mole said to himself, reflecting again on Prince Berrian, "is the kind of king who never wears a crown without a reason."

While Moleander was adjusting a bench along a table, something clattered at the other end of the room. Mole paused and looked up. The door at the end of the Upper Hall opened, but although a shaft of dust-flecked light from the corridor spilled through the opening, he could see no one.

"Hello?" he probed, straightening.

A shadow shifted beneath the edge of the table. A man, little taller than the back of a chair, appeared in the patch of sunlight near the door. "Hello," he returned. "They told me I might find you here, Moleander."

Mole blinked, then smiled. "Gwarthan! I didn't see you at first, there behind the chair, and it took me a minute to recognize you. It's been two years since I've seen you. I heard you'd broken the spell that confined you to your tower, so when I heard you were coming to the council, I expected you'd be—"

"Taller?" the enchanter hazarded. He coughed and brushed at a bit of lint on his light blue sleeve. "Well, if you must know, I *was* taller, at least back to my normal height, when I first left Eber Ystadun. But after all those years of being small, I found that I'd grown fond of being short. Being tall is so cumbersome, you know. It is—as one only finds out when one has been small for a number of years—more convenient to be short."

Mole folded his arms and glanced at the rafters. "I suppose it is pleasant not to be forced to watch out for doorframes and beams."

"Indeed, but that's only the beginning of it. When a person is large, he constantly worries about finding chairs with plenty of room for his legs, beds that are long enough to stretch out on, and so forth. No, being tall is much too much of a nuisance."

"Whatever size you are, Gwarthan," Mole said, "it's good to have you here. It makes it like—old times."

To this the wizard scratched his head. "It must be a blow to see me, then," he reckoned, slowly, "because, as I remember them, old times were not so happy. The last time I saw you, Moleander, you were on your way to face death at Caeodd."

Mole suppressed a shiver at the mention of Caeodd, the briar-hedged ruin where he had met and slain the black sorcerer Ammar. "What I mean," he said, "is that your coming will stir things up around here. You've no idea how troublesome this peaceful life of picking apples and learning poems is getting to be. There's a saying about you, Gwarthan. You're called the War Horn of Thrinedor in all the books, because every time you come here, war follows."

"That's a true name for me, but not a pleasant one. I did come to Thrinedor almost a hundred years ago to ask the warriors of Hwyl to come to Northmarch, for the greatest battle of our age. My coming is little less urgent now, and there may indeed be war. Perhaps before spring. Why do you smile, Moleander? Do you *want* war?"

Mole shook his head. "Of course not. Nobody in his right mind *wants* war. But I do want a change, some excitement. A war might make for a little adventure."

Gwarthan's eyebrows dropped. "Adventure, eh? Trouble, rather. I assure you that I will propose no adventures to the council tonight. I've come to warn of a growing peril—"

"Peril and adventure are about the same thing," Mole countered. "At least, you really can't have one without the other."

Instead of replying, Gwarthan peered out the window and tugged at his beard. King Ellarwy's two youngest sons were playing tag in the courtyard below; their shouts lifted lazily up the sun-warmed stones of the castle.

Mole pushed his bench aside and joined the wizard at the window. "I've heard rumors about what's happening on Fellheath. But I can't believe them."

Eyes fixed on the downs beyond the castle wall, Gwarthan remained silent for a time. "I, too, didn't believe the first whispers about sorcery rising in the north. I thought the same tales you have heard to be distorted observations of over-vivid imaginations. But the most horrifying gossip you've heard is true and is not the worst of what is going on in Vivrandon. I know. I've been there."

"To Vivrandon?"

"To Rathvidrian itself."

Stooping toward Gwarthan, Mole drew a great breath through his teeth. "Tell me," he said.

For a moment Gwarthan's eyes clamped to Mole's, but then the enchanter turned away to focus his attention on the games of the princes in the courtyard. "I wouldn't wish to dampen your afternoon, my boy," he said. "My tale is baleful enough to cast a shadow over the sun." Mole stood straighter in surprise as Gwarthan went on. "If I told you of Fellheath now, you'd be too upset to finish setting up the benches for the council, and Ellarwy would be furious. Besides, I've no time to rattle out the whole story. It will have to wait. In the meantime, I'd like to visit a friend or two at Avy-Ellarwch.''

"My companions from Mon Ceth, you mean?"

"Who else?" The wizard turned to the window. "Might I find them at Avy-Ellarwch?"

"Some of them," Mole answered. "Fflad will be there, and so will Orne. But Llan is in the care of the masters at the Tutory. He fell from an apple tree yesterday."

Gwarthan's chin rose sharply. "Indeed? Has he broken something?"

"The masters can't tell, though they don't think so." He shrugged and grinned. "But knowing Llan, he is probably up by now, playing pranks with Orne."

"What about our loremaster, Gareth?"

"He won't be *our* loremaster much longer." Mole sighed. "He's taken it into his head to leave Thrinedor; he's been hired by the King of Sharicom and will be leaving after the council, perhaps tomorrow. But you ought to find him at Avy-Ellarwch. I left him there this morning."

Gwarthan nodded. But he took only two steps toward the door before turning to look at Mole keenly, hand half-raised. "Just a minute, Moleander," he said. "I think we've left out one of your old friends."

"One of my friends?" Mole returned. "I don't think so."

"Yes we have. Arien."

Mole's lips twitched slightly. "Oh yes," he said. "Arien. I don't know how I forgot her—"

"When all of you came to my tower, Arien didn't seem easy to forget. I have found myself remembering her on my travels whenever I met a beautiful woman. But more, I've been thinking about her book, the one your old guardian Rhawn gave her. I have an inkling about both the book and the girl and how they fit together. And how your Arien is a part of what is happening on Fellheath. Of all your friends, she is the one with whom I *must* speak. Do you know where I might find her?"

Mole looked down at the sun-splashed flagstones.

"Come," the wizard prompted. "Is she at Avy-Ellarwch?"

In silence Mole placed his foot on a bench. "No," he said in a voice just above a whisper. "She's not."

A shade of understanding crossed Gwarthan's face. But still he asked, "You've no idea where she is?"

Mole's foot slammed to the floor. The harshness of his own reply surprised him. "How would I know where she is? Am I her father? For all I know"—his last words grated in his throat—"for all I know, Arien could be goblin-hunting on horseback in the Mon Dau!"

As the afternoon aged, Mole finished his work in the Upper Hall and went to see Wildfoal, the horse the High King had given him two years before. When he crossed the courtyard, he saw a cloud grope across the sky and curl, like a winter leaf, into itself. A pale belt of fire flickered over the west towers; it cast a baleful light on the battlements and a sombre shadow across the castle square.

He spent nearly an hour in the stable, pushing a brush against Wildfoal's back. Although the stable masters had groomed all the horses that morning, Mole cleaned Wildfoal with care. It was pleasant to feel the solid warmth of the horse's sides, to see the pearl gleam of his mane. Mole had always considered the stable the next-most exciting part of Ranath Thrine after the armory; it smelled of horses and oats and hay and also of saddles and wind and wet earth. It helped him remember what the world was like beyond the study rooms, courtyards, and orchards of Ranath Thrine.

While he worked, he contemplated the upcoming council. But his thoughts soon drifted to other things, to a face, both beautiful and painful, that peered at him from a seat on an ice-colored stallion.

"Bother," he said to himself. He plunged his brush into his pail and began stroking anew.

He soon noticed the crimson sunset fading from the cracks of the roof. With sudden urgency, he replaced the brush in the bucket, patted Wildfoal good-bye, and jogged from the stable back into the courtyard.

He ought not be late for the council.

Most of the invited nobles had assembled in the Upper Hall by the time Mole arrived. But although the benches were

filled, a feeling of emptiness thickened the air. A torch flared
on either side of the doorway, casting long, unsteady shadows
over the hall. The only other light came from a small blaze
on a hearth and from the moon, which burned coldly like a
candle behind frosty glass; it greyed the faces and hands of
those seated along the windows. Only clasped hands adorned
the long, bare tables; no meat or wine would be served until
the council was done. No banners fluttered from the rafters,
no bright insignias shone from the dim walls above the
benches. A curious smell, or absence of it, hovered like smoke
beneath the glare of the torches. Only the voice of the fire
hissed in the silence; even Mole's own footfalls seemed to
boom. His eyes swept across the tables. Nobles from Thrinedor were seated at the first table, the one nearest the hearth.
Envoys from the outlands gathered around the second. Mole
saw that his place would be at the third table, the one nearest
the doors, where slumped a few of the lesser captains of
Thrinedor and a prince from the frontiers.

Mole glided to a seat near the end of the bench, next to a
thick captain whose name he could not remember.

As soon as Mole sat down, a man, clad in a long green man-
tle strode into the room. The man paused between the torches,
sniffed at his cuff, then moved toward the head table. Prince
Berrian. At once Mole's eyebrows lowered.

"Berrian!" Mole whispered loudly.

The prince's face swung toward him.

"Berrian!" Mole repeated. "Come here!"

Prince Berrian cast a glance in the direction of the first
table, then approached Mole.

"What is it?"

Mole looked at Prince Berrian's wheat-colored hair bunch-
ing against his high collar. "I was looking for you earlier today, Berrian," he began coolly. "Your father wanted me to
ready these tables, and he suggested that you might help me.
But you weren't anywhere around—"

"It's foolish to seek help from the crown prince on the day
of a council," Berrian said. He raised his chin to regard the
thin shadows threading along the walls. "I've been abysmally
busy today."

"That I don't doubt. Were you running errands?"

Prince Berrian nodded swiftly.

"On horseback perhaps?" Mole persisted.

Berrian swung his shoulder away. "I don't see," he said with sudden fierceness, "why I should suffer myself to be interrogated by you. What I do is my business and none of yours."

"It becomes my business," Mole said, teeth fixed, "when it has to do with Arien."

"So that's it, is it?" Eyes blazing, Berrian threw Mole a scathing smile. "Who are you, Moleander? Arien's brother? No. Arien's father?" Berrian's eyes fell toward Mole's tunic. "Rather you are Arien's horsemaster by the look of you!"

The torchlight revealed shining strands of Wildfoal's mane on Mole's sleeves. Turning scarlet, he stifled an urge to brush the hair from his arms. He wanted to retort, but the prince, with a grin, had already turned away. Without another look in Mole's direction, Berrian stalked to a seat in a chair on his father's right.

Mole almost forgot his anger when he saw King Ellarwy. Even in the ruddy light from the torches, the king's cheeks were ashen, bloodless, drawn disturbingly tight across his face. Disquieting flames fluttered on the mirrors of his eyes.

A premonition shook Mole and he shifted his glance from where Berrian smoothed his bangs to where King Ellarwy, with Gwarthan at his side, rose from his high-backed chair to face the assembly.

The last patter of conversation withered.

"Men of Thrinedor," King Ellarwy began, "lords from over the Thrine, good friends. You have all been summoned here for a council in a time of great unrest and danger. You will forgive, I trust, my lack of formality. But we are not here to exchange pleasantries. We are not here to drink or to feast or to make merry. We have come here to counsel. We have come to speak of war."

A murmur hummed above the crackle of the torches, then died.

"But before we can speak of war, we must hear of what we must do battle against. None of us here are ignorant of the threat in Vivrandon, yet none of us know more of it than the shadows we have seen on our porches and the tales we have heard in our halls. Only one man among us has been to Fellheath and has seen for himself what malice grows there.''

Mole's attention shifted to Gwarthan, whose frown mirrored Ellarwy's. It occurred to Mole that the enchanter must be standing on his chair, for his face was as high as the king's; at the same time, Mole had the impression that Gwarthan had grown to a tremendous height. His teeth were clenched, and his eyes threw specks of fire as he observed the council.

"I have seen Vivrandon. And what I have seen I don't wish to tell you, though I must. If the tale of the corruption of Vivrandon is to be told, it must begin with the coming of people to the North. We were unlike any of the creatures who had formerly inhabited these northern countries; we were neither wholly corrupt, like the wolfmen and goblins, nor completely innocent, like the deer and bears. Instead, we were changeable and uncommitted, caught in a maelstrom between Good and Evil. Garren Mehridene, the first High King, covenanted with the Emperor, Master of the North, that he and his people after him would always defend Good—''

"We need no lesson in history," said one of the lords of Northmarch. "All of us know of King Garren's oath.''

"Ah, you know *of* it. But you do not *know* it. Indeed, few but Garren and his descendants have heeded that oath. Many men have estranged themselves from the oath and have turned to darkness—''

"There has always been darkness," someone from Mole's table pointed out. "And there will always be those who choose it.''

"Naturally, sir. There always have been breakers of Garren's oath. But never before has Garren's own blood denied his covenant.''

Mole's eyes lowered to a splash of fire on the stones near King Ellarwy's feet. At least one of the whispers Mole had heard was now confirmed.

"Yes," Gwarthan went on, frowning, "Ichodred of Vivrandon has denied the oath. He has chosen darkness. And all of Vivrandon has chosen it with him. You are not so astounded as you pretend to be, my lords. This darkness isn't new. It has been brooding, groping to power in Vivrandon for many years. It takes time to corrupt Garren's blood. When the royal house of Vivrandon began with the first hawk king, Fifran, son of Llarandil the Great, Fellheath was as happy as Thrinedor. But when Fifran perished at Northmarch defending his brother, a sadness came to Fellheath that has not yet left it. Fifran II, Fifran's son, was called King of Tears. But if his tears were sorrow, tears in Ranath Vivrandon have since turned to anger.

"True evil accompanied the son of Fifran II, Ichodron, to the throne. In the days of Ichodron, Pesten was cloaked under the sorcery of Ammar. Thrinedor was thrown at bay, being so near the holds of the Dark One. The other kingdoms—Crywyll, Sharicom, and Aelenwaith—busied themselves with refugees from the Pestene trading cities along the River Ystadun. So Vivrandon became the most powerful realm in the North. Ichodron's warriors numbered in the thousands."

The enchanter's face dipped into a blotch of darkness. "At the peak of King Ichodron's might, his mother, Rhea, Lady Fellflood, died or at least departed Fellheath forever. She was the last influence for good in Ranath Vivrandon. Ichodron soon fell prey to his own pride. His riders were the swiftest in the Kingdoms, his forges most hot with sword iron. And in time he regarded with envy the seat of the High King at Ranath Drallm. The time has come for the heathland to rule the woodland, he thought. So he waited and watched while his hosts swelled and became more skilled in the arts of war.

"A few years ago, about the time Ammar was overthrown in Pesten, King Ichodron was murdered. To the hawk throne came a moody youth named Ichodred. He was the very image of his father, I am told, dark and strong. And unfortunately he shared more of his father's pride than was good for him. Furthermore not only did he delight in his armies, but he also had a taste for sorcery. Only last winter he brought to Rathvidrian (his new name for Ranath Vivrandon) a warlock of the same school as was Ammar. This necromancer is nameless, called only the Black Counselor. But the sound of his magic drums in Fellheath's rocks cries with the hawks of

Vivrandon and creeps across the Thrinefens—toward us."

Mole adjusted himself in his seat. A creak from the boards below him snapped several pairs of eyes in his direction.

"This is grim news, Gwarthan." One of the dark-skinned underlords from Sharicom rose with the customary nod toward the king. "But I do not see that the matter needs discussion. Our path is plain. We must gather our warriors at once and take war into Vivrandon before the snows set in."

"You men of Sharicom are herdsmen, not farmers," the captain next to Mole shouted. "You have no apples to pick, no wheat to thresh. Our folk of Thrinedor harvest with the first flakes as it is, without marching to war. Consider the number of warriors the hawk king has. If you wish to seize Rathvidrian, you must wait until Thrinedor can muster to aid you. That will be spring."

"We of Sharicom have never cowered waiting for allies," the underlord returned, crisply. "King Cashma has already sounded for war."

"You must urge your king to wait, then," King Ellarwy broke in. The pale outthrust of his jaw silenced the underlord's protest. "Though the High King has sent no emissaries to this council, he knows of the broken oath in Vivrandon and plans to move against Ichodred when the frost breaks. Further, he commands that no realm, particularly Sharicom, violate the frontiers of Vivrandon until then. Remind your king that the warriors of Pesten, as well, are farmers to whom winter is an enemy more fearsome and deadly than anything that could come out of Fellheath. My lord, you must advise King Cashma to hold his wrath until after planting in the spring."

"I will inform him of the High King's wishes," the underlord replied stiffly, "but I can't guarantee that my words will restrain him. He is a man of strong will. Outlaws from Vivrandon have already raided our keeps in the north wolds; our people are angry enough that already we can raise a host larger than the one High King Gion brought against Ammar two years ago—"

"Ichodred is not Ammar," someone Mole could not see said. "I've heard that Vivrandon employs few goblins. Most

of Ichodred's regiments are mounted men, grey riders of the
Hawk King. These are more than a match for any number of
shepherds!''

"Are farmers swifter with the sword?" the Sharicom lord
answered, flushing with rage.

"Come!" King Ellarwy's voice rang out above the wave of
bickering from the second table. "Come! Peace! My lord of
Sharicom, your king, no matter how angry, doesn't have a
choice. No king may attack one of the other kingdoms without
the sanction of the High King. Admonish Cashma to stay on
his own side of the River Woldwash if he values his crown."

The noble nodded but threw a dark glance at his comrade.

"One moment," Gwarthan said. "I haven't finished my ac-
count of the doings in Vivrandon. I've yet much to say that
may dissuade King Cashma from impetuous movement."

Gwarthan paused, as if to be certain all were listening.

"You all have reckoned of goblins and men, of horsemen
and warriors, but you've left out something very important.
Have you forgotten Ammar already? The greatest threat that
Ichodred presents is not his army; it is his Black Counselor.
For there is some sorcery at work in Fellflood Vale that sur-
passes even the most potent of Ammar's spells."

"The Book of Gath!" Mole shouted, with a sudden
memory of the horrible night at the ruins of Ranath Caeodd.
"The Black Counselor has it!"

The enchanter's gaze touched him. "Truly a devastating
thought. But no, Moleander. That tool of black magic was
removed from the vaults of Caeodd this very summer. The
High King has hidden it again beneath Ranath Drallm. It is
away from evil hands."

Recoiling, Mole ignored Berrian's smiling stare. Mole had
known the Book had been taken to Drallm. The fact, frustrat-
ingly, had momentarily skipped his mind. "What is the
danger, then?"

"The danger," Gwarthan answered, mysteriously, "is that
we don't know exactly what the danger is."

"Whatever do you mean?" Ellarwy asked.

Gwarthan's features blanched to the color of the moonlight
on the windows. "As I have said, my news from Vivrandon is

first hand. I was there. I spied for almost two weeks in Fellflood Vale. I was invisible, of course. When I had collected enough information, I started up the river toward the village of Fellhaven, from which I hoped to reach Thrinedor. I was creeping north of the river, in the Fell Downs, so as to avoid Ichodred's riders. I was not particularly concerned about my safety; I had moved unchecked up until that time, and if I came on any warriors, I would have plenty of spells to defend myself.

"A rider, all in black and grey, with a hawk on his shoulder, overtook me halfway to Fellhaven. He was no ghost, no sorcerer, merely a man. By the look of his nose, he was one of the hawk lords of Vivrandon. I saw him before he saw me, so when he was near enough, I sprang from behind a stone and cast on him one of my very best curses.

"But nothing happened!" Gwarthan's eyes went wide. "Nothing! Certainly, the man's horse became a chunk of granite, but he went unscathed. While he drew his sword, I hurled another spell, one that once vaporized a dozen necromancers. But still nothing happened. Never before has any black magic protected a man so thoroughly from the incantations of the House of the Sky."

A nearby nobleman voiced Mole's thoughts. "Perhaps a new evil has come into the world."

"Perhaps. But more likely the rider was protected by some power of Good that has been twisted around by the Black Counselor of Vivrandon. Only certain forms of white magic could have preserved that warrior from my spell. If evil manipulates good enchantments, we are truly helpless."

"We have our swords!" Berrian objected.

Gwarthan cocked an eyebrow. "I had mine in the Fell Downs, and I drew it. But although three of my blows pierced the rider's guard and one of them his chest, he was not hurt. He shouted at me something about being watched over by the power of the Fellflood. Whatever kept him, I could not slay him. I escaped only by becoming invisible and running. He was invincible. Deathless."

"That's impossible!"

"I thought so, too. But I couldn't kill him. As frightened as

I was, I wanted an explanation. I returned to the war camps under the walls of Rathvidrian. I netted testing spells over all the valley to determine whether others were protected by this vile sorcery."

A breathless silence filled the Upper Hall.

King Ellarwy asked, steadily, "There were others?"

Gwarthan slowly nodded.

"How many?"

Gwarthan paused and swallowed. "I counted fewer than a hundred. It seems that only those with ties to the Royal House of Vivrandon have been protected."

"A hundred is enough," growled one of the frontier lords. "I daresay even *one* deathless man could make much mischief for us. In fact, we have no chance of defeating Vivrandon, if, as you say, it has deathless warriors in its employ."

A murmur of agreement rose.

"We've no chance at present, yes," Gwarthan shouted over the rumble. "Why do you think we've chosen to wait until spring to march? In the meantime I and a few of my associates will return to Fellflood Vale and break the spell or at least find out who's responsible for it!"

"But you said yourself you haven't the vaguest idea of how the spell was cast!" muttered a lord from Northmarch.

"What if you should fail in both your efforts?"

"What if you find that the spell is stronger than you are? You could do nothing against it in the Fell Downs. What makes you think you'll be able to do more this winter?"

Lines tightened on Gwarthan's brow. "It seems to me," he said, "that all of that is my problem. Your problem, as has already been stated, is to muster to march in spring. As far as the deathless riders of Vivrandon are concerned, I'm confident that I'll be able to disarm their enchanted shields. For there is a prophecy—"

"There are many prophecies. But not all have come true."

"But this one will," Gwarthan retorted. "This prediction comes from one of the wisest men ever to live in the Kingdoms, a man who should know more of Vivrandon than any of us here. Fifran, the first king in Fellflood Vale, spoke it to his brothers, Hwyl and Strein, before he perished at the Battle of Northmarch. Although it, like many prophecies, is puzzling, it spells the certain destruction of the evil power burgeoning now in Vivrandon.

> "When the hawks of Fellheath cry,
> When Vivrandon burns,
> The prince shall be a slave;
> The knave shall be a prince.
> The lifeless shall find life
> And the deathless find death."

A lull quieted all voices but those of the torches.

"Indeed, Gwarthan," King Ellarwy said huskily, "these words speak of our time. When Vivrandon burns—that is, when we bring war onto the heaths—the cursed spell shall break. But there is much more I don't understand. There is much that troubles me. The lifeless find life? What, with our coming to Fellheath, will the graves open so that Ichodred may lead a wraith-host against us?"

"I don't know," Gwarthan replied. "We'll have to risk such things as that."

Fingers curved into his beard, King Ellarwy nodded. "Let's argue no more about magic." He addressed the assembly. "Enchantments have a way of carrying out themselves. Instead let us prepare for war with the coming of spring."

"But what do we do now, Your Majesty?" asked one of the underlords from Sharicom. "King Cashma won't like to be idle. It wouldn't be wise for you to do nothing, either. Raiders from Fellheath may cross the River Thrine just as they've crossed the Woldwash."

King Ellarwy considered. "I won't violate Vivrandon's borders. I hope King Cashma will do the same. Yet," he went on, "I won't leave my own side of the Thrine unguarded. I'll organize a force, a group of no more than a dozen horsemen, to patrol the river after the first snow falls, when raids are more likely to occur."

"I, gladly, would ride with these men," called out one of the young Thrinedor captains.

King Ellarwy nodded. "One of the twelve is chosen."

Immediately four more captains volunteered for the task.

"Come, men of Thrinedor," Gwarthan said after a moment of silence. "To be one of the twelve winter riders is not such a grim thing." Gwarthan looked at Mole. "It's not war yet. Rather it should almost be an adventure."

Mole had nearly spoken out before all the others, but something, some annoying worry, had dried the words in the back of his throat. He could already see the blue ice of the River Thrine between him and the rises of Fellheath. He could smell the snap of ice in the wind and the scent of horse and iron below him. It would be an adventure, indeed, an adventure as cold, dangerous, and refreshing as Mole's excursions onto the slopes of Misty Mountain had been.

Yet, maddeningly, Llan's face pushed itself over Mole's snow-sprinkled imagination. Mole could not be sure of how long Llan would be sick. As long as Llan was bedridden, Mole must be near. And there was Gareth to be thought of—Gareth would be leaving within a few days.

Five more men committed themselves to the guard.

"Some of you are worried about your fields and orchards. But I tell you that the white guard will not leave Ranath Thrine until after the first snow, when all of your crops have been gathered in. The folk of Vivrandon will be harvesting—and not raiding—until then. Now, we've room for two more." King Ellarwy swept the hall with his eyes. "Only two more riders, for I want a vanguard, not an army."

The thick-limbed man next to Mole lifted his arm.

"Very good, Rhan," the king said. "One more, now."

Mole bit the end of his tongue. Winter, he thought. By the first snow Llan will be well. The scars of Gareth's departure will have healed. None of the others, not even Fflad and Arien, he knew, would grudge him an adventure by then. He was suddenly chilled by a notion of what Arien might think of him if he *didn't* go.

"I'll go!" he shouted, lifting his eyes. "I'll go!"

But he saw that a hand had gone up with his, that another voice mingled with his outcry.

Berrian's eyes flew to Mole; the two locked in a glare. "I spoke first," Berrian said.

"I think they volunteered at once," Gwarthan said.

King Ellarwy seemed to note the heat in both pairs of eyes.

"Now, Berrian. Moleander. Both of you can't go. I want no more than twelve to ride the river. One of you—whoever is the most noble—must decline."

"I won't," Mole returned. "I'm going!"

"He isn't!" Berrian countered. He looked up at King Ellarwy. "Father, you must allow me. I wish to go. I yearn to go." Berrian flung a look at Mole. "In fact," Berrian continued, "I *demand* to go. Have you forgotten that I'm your crown prince? When I take the realm—years from now—I must have experience in such things, as you had in your youth. Has the law and tradition of Thrinedor slipped your mind? One of the titles of the heir to the throne is that of Horn-Bearer. How can I bear the war horn of Thrinedor if I wait in the castle like a child?"

King Ellarwy avoided looking at both his son and Mole. "So be it." He sighed. "Berrian shall go, then. Moleander, I'm sorry to disappoint you. But I assure you that if any of the riders find cause to remain home, you will be the first to take his place."

"Thank you, sire," Mole said, eyes cast down, lips drawn across his teeth in suppressed fury. "I will be ready if you need me."

When Mole looked up again, Berrian was arranging his hair around his ears. As he saw Mole watching him, he only smiled and began talking to the nobleman next to him.

·3·

Rain

MOLE thought as he approached the gates of Avy-Ellarwch that the moon looked as if it were made of snow. It threw a waxy light on the path; it made the roofs of the castle glint uneasily above the squares of lighted windows.

Although it was not cold, Mole thrust his fists into the pockets of his tunic. Snow. Snow wouldn't be long in coming. "Bother," he said aloud. "Blast Prince Berrian, blast the twelve riders, and blast adventure itself!" He reconsidered his last curse. "I shall make my own adventure," he decided. "I'll go goblin-hunting in the north or outlaw-battling in the Thrinefens. By the Emperor, I'll do anything but waste away in this blasted castle all winter!" His purpose thus stated, he began to relax as he made the final turn in the trail.

He halted.

"Arien," he said as soon as he recognized the robed figure in the light from the Tutory windows. The girl stood in the gateway, clutching one of the gate bars.

"Mole," she said. "I . . . I didn't think you'd be back so soon." She added, almost accusingly, "I thought you were going to curry Wildfoal."

"I had time before," he replied. He moved toward her.

Arien glanced away into the darkness.

Mole hesitated. "Aren't you coming in?" He frowned. "I haven't seen you all day. I'd like to talk to you about something. We can talk on the way to the Tutory; we really ought to pay Llan a visit."

"Visit Llan?" Arien said absently. "Yes, do that, Mole. He'll love to see you. The masters say he's had a fever; it broke a few hours ago, but he's feeling melancholy—"

"Aren't you coming?" Mole broke in.

"I was just with him," Arien said.

Mole turned to her. He squared his hands on his hips and narrowed his eyes. "If I didn't know better," he began, "I'd say that you're trying to get rid of me. More than that, I'd think you were waiting for somebody, out so late by the gate."

"I *was* waiting for somebody," Arien returned. "I was waiting for you. And here you are. Now stop looking at me like that and go to see Llan. I'll join you after I catch a breath or two of air." Arien assumed an uneasy frown. "Honestly, Mole! What's wrong with you. Has all the suspicious talk from that council gone to your head?"

"There was plenty to be suspicious about at the council," Mole said. "And there's plenty to be suspicious about here, too."

Arien pressed her lips in rage. She swung away to face the darkness.

"Are you going or not?" she demanded at length.

"Not. I need a breath of air as much as you do after that council. We can talk just as well here as we could anywhere else."

"I don't feel like talking to you, Moleander Ammarbane." She tossed her head. "Go on, now."

Although Mole made no retort, he did not leave. He moved to the stone post of the gate, leaned against it, and folded his arms. Arien pretended not to notice him; she paced, her skirts brushing against the heads of the grass along the edge of the hill.

"Whoa!" a voice came from the darkness. Then, "Good evening, Arien."

Arien edged toward the horse with a backward glance. "Berrian," she whispered. "You've brought it?"

"Would I come without it?" The prince beamed.

Arien did not answer. Mole, in the shadow of the gate post, remained still.

Without taking his eyes from Arien, Prince Berrian reached into the breast of his tunic. He produced something that Mole could identify only as a fold of burlap. He handed it to Arien.

"Thank you," Arien said. "You're very kind."

" 'Twas nothing," Berrian returned. He steadied his horse. "I told you, my mother has rooms full of it. Shall I bring you more?"

Arien squeezed the package between her palms. "No. This will do nicely. But I appreciate the offer."

"Can I bring you something else, then? Needles, perhaps?"

Arien considered.

"Whatever you'll need for winter you must ask me for now," Berrian said. "For I will be gone with the first snow. I've been chosen to lead a regiment that will be patrolling the river—"

Mole burst from the shadows, pushed Arien aside, and faced Berrian. "Liar!" he shouted. "Chosen to lead the river riders? Ha! If your father were not king of Thrinedor, you'd have not even been invited to the council!"

Berrian's horse started and wheeled. Some minutes passed before the prince could steady the horse enough to retort, "Sneak! Lurking in the shadows! How dare you eavesdrop? How dare you speak to me like that!"

Arien caught Mole's elbow. "Please, Mole!"

He jerked his arm from her grasp. "Sneak yourself! Wheedling your father about being crown prince!"

"But I am crown prince," Berrian sneered. "And you're not. You're not much more than a horsemaster!"

Mole snatched Berrian's reign. "We'll see who is better, the horsemaster or the prince. Come down from your saddle, and I'll take my fists to you!"

Tearing away from Mole's grip, Berrian urged his horse down the road. "You dare threaten me? By the three sorcerers, I'd love to rip you apart, limb from limb. But I am a prince, not a common boy to roll in the dirt. And I won't abase myself before this lady. If you want to have it out with me, bring a sword to Ranath Thrine, and I will disarm you, as

I did in the games.'' Mole clenched his teeth but thwarted the impulse to fly at Berrian. "As for you, Arien," Berrian called out, turning his horse, "I'm sorry for my savage conduct. I'll bring you needles tomorrow."

Before Mole could sputter a taunt after him, Berrian vanished into the night.

Mole whirled toward the gate. "Not waiting for anyone, eh?"

Arien's cheeks whitened with fury. She clutched the burlap package to her breast.

"Presents from the prince?"

"Mole! Stop it at once. I've had quite enough."

"*You've* had quite enough? *You?* Don't tell *me* you've had enough. You lied to me. You wanted to keep me from knowing that you were to have a rendezvous with that arrogant princeling."

"I knew you wouldn't understand!"

"Understand? I think I understand perfectly. I think I know now what you've been doing in your spare afternoons and on the nights Enna sees you creep in late."

Arien's eyes glinted with tears. "Oooh!" she burst out. "If you only knew! If you only knew! Blast your silly jealousy! Blast your silly pride! You think you're so much better than Berrian! You do! But let me tell you something. He's twice the man you are. You act like a silly child, taunting at him like that, threatening a fist fight!"

"He provoked me! Did you hear what he said? Are you deaf?"

"I'm not deaf," Arien returned, "so I don't need to be yelled at. At least *he* didn't shout at me!"

Mole sprang forward and plucked the burlap packet from Arien. She squeaked with anger as the cloth unfolded and its contents spilled to the ground.

Mole froze. The moonlight revealed several skeins of embroidery thread scattered on the earth.

Arien wasted no time in kneeling and gathering them into the piece of burlap, which she demanded of Mole with a frown. She pushed the bundle under her arm and stalked toward the gate.

Mole followed her with his stare.

"If you weren't an old friend," she said icily, "I'd never speak to you again." She slipped into the night, leaving a single bundle of thread on the threshold of the gate, pale against the night-dark stones.

Mole did not bother to pick it up when he passed.

Because he didn't want to grope for a candle, Mole undressed in the dark.

A single moonbeam lit his fingers as he fought to untie the cord at the throat of his tunic. "By the Emperor," he hissed, jerking at the knot, "I can't understand it!"

"Understand what?" broke in the voice of the Sword. It shimmered on its hooks but spoke quietly.

"Everything!" Mole answered in a thick whisper. "This whole day. First Enna, then the council, then that braggart Berrian. But Arien was the worst of it. I can't understand that girl!"

"I never could, either," said the Sword sympathetically. "Your Arien and I have never gotten along, not since the day she called me a worthless chip of iron. She's turned on *you* now, has she?"

Mole bit his lip. He pulled his tunic over his head.

"She's bound to get over it," the Sword soothed.

Clouds blotted the stars beyond the window. "But what I don't see," Mole said, "is what I did that was so wrong! I'll admit I got nasty when Prince Berrian showed up. But I was polite enough before. It was almost as if Arien thought herself a martyr, as if she'd met Berrian for my sake, not hers."

"Maybe she did," the Sword submitted.

Fumbling to find his bed, Mole rejected the idea at once.

"Oh, before you go to sleep, my boy, I've something to tell you."

"Go ahead." Mole drew the blankets aside. "If it's good news, it will cheer me up, and if it's bad, I won't be surprised."

"The others are asleep. At least they were. They would have waited up for you, but it's late, and Gareth is supposed to go to Ranath Thrine at dawn—"

"He's got to go to Sharicom? So soon?"

"Apparently. But at any rate, you should go to sleep at

once. And I suggest you shutter the window if you want to get any rest. A storm is moving in from the highlands.''

Mole sniffed the darkness. "There isn't any wind," he said. "And there are only a few clouds."

"Suit yourself, my boy," the Sword said cheerfully. "Rain doesn't bother me!"

"I never dreamed it would rain," Mole said to Llan, "not even when the Sword told me it would. But look at it now!" The rain indeed came down in grey streaks beyond the window. It dropped in sheets off the Tutory eaves and splashed against the bright stones of the courtyard.

"I *knew* it was going to rain," Llan said from his bed. "I knew it all along." He locked his teeth. "Beastly stuff!"

Mole moved from the window to the cot. Llan watched him with eyes the color of a washed-out sky. His cheeks, waxy and almost transparent, tightened when he saw Mole looking at him. "You won't let me say good-bye to Gareth, will you?" he accused.

"Nonsense. Of course you'll say good-bye to him." Mole's fingers rested briefly on Llan's forehead. Hairlines of pain, like writing on parchment, marked Llan's brow. "You'll say good-bye to Gareth," Mole repeated, "but you won't see him off. Orne's waiting downstairs. I'll send him to bring Gareth here before he goes to Ranath Thrine."

A fit of coughing broke Llan's groan of protest. "But that isn't the same at all," he said. "And it isn't fair!"

"Certainly not fair. But wise."

Llan's head sunk back against the pillow. "It's all the rain's fault. I knew the rain would ruin everything!"

"Even if it weren't raining, you couldn't walk all the way to Ranath Thrine. You still couldn't see Gareth off."

"I couldn't walk," Llan retorted. "But somebody could carry me." He sized Mole with his eyes. "You're strong enough, Mole. You're strong enough to lift me, blankets and all—"

"If you're suggesting that I take you out in the rain," Mole said, "I won't do it. I can't do it. The masters want you here at the Tutory for a good reason. They want you to get well. So do I. Besides," Mole added, glancing at the stairs, "Arien would have my head if I took you into the rain."

"Arien wants your head already, from what I hear."

Mole's eyes fell to the floorboards.

"I'm sorry," Llan said quickly. "Now, please take me, Mole."

Shaking his head, Mole turned to the window.

"Please. *Please.* I'd be dry enough. I'd bring plenty of blankets. And I know you're strong enough. Come on, Mole. Please, *please!*"

Mole did not look at Llan. "Roll your blankets around you, then. Put them over your face as well. I wouldn't ever forgive myself if your cough got worse or if you caught cold."

Mole thrust his arms underneath Llan's body, hoisted him into his arms, and walked toward the stairs with his back arched, feet blind. "Oh, thank you, Mole." Llan sighed as Mole edged his way down the steps. Mole, however, did not reply; already his forearms ached. And at every jolt, Llan suppressed a groan.

"Llan's coming?" asked Orne, who was at the bottom of the stairs. He joined Mole near the door to the courtyard.

"It looks like it, doesn't it?" Mole said.

"How nice!" Orne clapped his hands. But his features soon darkened, and he asked in a voice just above a whisper, "Are you feeling all right, Llan?"

Llan seemed to battle an impulse to cough. "I'm better," he said, but the gruffness in his voice cast a frown onto Orne's face.

"Orne," Mole grunted, "open the door please."

After a moment's hesitation, Orne obeyed.

But through the doorway came not only the spray of rain but also Arien, who wore raindrops on her face and a grimace on her lips. She froze when she saw Mole.

"And just what do you think you're doing?"

"He's bringing Llan to see Gareth leave," Orne answered.

Arien narrowed her eyes. "He is, is he?"

"Come on, Ari," Mole said between his teeth. "He's well-wrapped. And he'll soon be back to dry blankets."

"But we can't take the chance. Put him back to bed, and I'll bring Gareth here."

"I won't," Mole said. He knew his cheeks were flushing. "I

promised Llan that he could see Gareth leave, and I'll keep my promise." With this he pushed past Arien, and with Orne in trail he started through the door.

By the time he reached the gate of Avy-Ellarwch, he heard footfalls in the puddles behind him. He glanced back and saw Arien, who looked at him with a deep frown. For an answer, he merely pushed on into the rain and told Orne to tuck in the blankets around Llan's feet.

The jog around the hilltop would have been more bearable for Mole without his two companions. Orne hindered his progress by constantly rearranging Llan's blankets; thus Mole was obliged to stop and steady his hold every few paces. Arien followed at some distance behind, and Mole fancied he could feel her eyes on his neck.

Fflad, Gareth, and the two underlords from Sharicom worked around three horses under the trees at the castle gate, where it was drier than it was out in the open. King Ellarwy, mantled heavily in green, tapped his foot nearby. A stout red pony was tied to the hedge on the far side of the road. A wet little man, whom Mole soon recognized as Gwarthan, stuffed a soaked book into the pony's saddlebags as Mole arrived.

"Good morning, Moleander, Arien," Gwarthan said cheerfully. "Good to have seen you both again."

Mole braced himself against a tree. He allowed Llan to settle lower in the crook of his arms. "You're leaving as well?"

"I've no time to waste. I've decided to go to Sharicom before I return to do some more spying at Rathvidrian. First, I want to see that your friend Gareth makes it to his new post as loremaster. (The roads across Fellheath and Northmarch are equally dangerous these days.) Then, I want to be sure King Cashma doesn't do anything rash. At least not before spring."

"I wish you a good journey, then. It may be a damp trek across Northmarch in this weather, though."

"True. But rain has never bothered me much." Gwarthan squeezed the water from his beard, which no longer seemed white.

"Rain bothers me," King Ellarwy growled, "and I'm not even going on a journey. If this pelting keeps up, it'll knock all the apples from the trees!"

Meanwhile Gareth and Fflad finished securing Gareth's belongings to the back of his horse. Both turned to the others, expectantly, Gareth forcing a frown.

"We'd better be off," he said.

"I don't see the hurry," Mole returned suddenly. "What's the rush? We could talk a bit. Or perhaps have a bit of breakfast in the castle."

"I've already had breakfast," Gareth said. He wrinkled his nose. "And I don't want to keep you all out here in this rain longer than I have to. Especially Llan, whom you've done no good by bringing here—"

"I wanted to come," Llan objected, thrusting his nose from the blankets. "Don't be in such a hurry to leave us."

"Yes," said Fflad. "We might not see you for a long time. Perhaps never again. I don't know about anybody else, but I'm going to miss . . ." Fflad's lip trembled when a raindrop struck it, "I'm going to miss . . . all that useful history you told me as background for my ballads. Confound it, I'm going to miss *you*."

"I'm going to miss you, too, and all that," Gareth answered. He thrust his arms into his pockets. "But it won't help to drag this out." His eyes darted toward the hedge, where the underlords and Gwarthan were mounting.

"Now the first thing you must do when you get to Ranath Sharicom," Arien admonished, "is find a seamstress to make you some presentable clothes. If I'd known what a sorry state yours were in, I'd have done so myself."

Whether he heard this or not, Gareth mounted his horse.

"Write us a message from Sharicom when you get there," Fflad said.

"Sleep under the trees tonight," Arien called out.

The company, Gwarthan in the lead, started down the road toward the fords. Once astride his horse, Gareth did not look back, though he echoed the shouts of farewell from Fflad and Arien.

"Good-bye," Mole managed to croak.

But his words were far too soft to be heard by anyone but Llan. They washed away into the thunder of the rain on the grass. Fflad and Arien, however, shouted after Gareth until they were hoarse, until the little knot of men, smudged by the rain, vanished into the willows along the Thrine.

Then no one spoke.

Presently Arien snatched Orne's hand and tugged him away
from the road. "If you want to drench yourself in the rain,"
she told Mole, coolly, "it's not my business. But I won't have
Llan in this for a moment longer. I'll take him back to bed if
you won't."

Eyes flickering with conflicting emotions, Mole staggered to
his feet from his half-seat against the tree. But his arms, he
found, had somehow become flaccid. He might have dropped
Llan had not Fflad propped his elbows at just the right moment.

"The blankets are heavy with rain," Mole said.

"Let me help you," Fflad offered. He hooked Llan's legs
over his arms, smiling slightly; understanding gleamed in his
eye. "The rain can make one's burden very heavy."

The days following Gareth's departure passed, damp and
drab. The rain slackened to a drizzle but refused to cease
altogether; it drummed relentlessly on the red roofs of Ranath
Thrine and darkened the straw roofs of Avy-Ellarwch. It
splashed endlessly against the stones of the courtyard, filling
first cracks, then hollows, then whole trenches. After a few
days, glossy pools ringed the courtyard. And although the
masters stopped the spigot of the fountain, the water spread to
the pool's edge and spilled over. The water reflected the leaves
of the mountain ash, which, polished by the daily rain, faded
to yellow, then ruddied to orange, then darkened to a brown
that matched the water beneath.

Beyond the walls of Avy-Ellarwch the trees went gold,
though the rain-fed mist often hid the orchards. A damp cold
arrived, a cheek-reddening chill that barred shutters and
clogged chimneys with dank-smelling smoke. The rain stopped
before each dawn long enough for frost to filigree the crum-
pling leaves and lid the puddles with ice.

These were long days for Mole, for he had little to do. He
had no chores. A troop of young orphans cleared the last
apples from the orchard the morning after the council. Few
other tasks remained now that the harvest was done. Chop-
ping wood. Fixing hinges or mending leaks, perhaps. But little

more. There were always studies, of course, but he couldn't seem to settle to them.

Fflad managed to occupy himself with his studies and his harping. Orne seemed restless, but when he wasn't visiting Llan, he, too, curled up near the fire with a book. For his part, Mole could stomach neither the company of books nor the smokiness of the bedchamber for very long. No matter how cold or damp it was outside, Mole did his best to avoid his room; the empty cots there reminded him of Gareth and Llan, and the Sword made him think of the adventures he was missing.

At first Mole spent dutiful hours with Llan. But the upper room of the Tutory soon seemed little less confining than the bedchamber. Llan, in addition, became increasingly poor company. He tried to be entertained by Mole's stories and conversation, but it was plain that he heard little of what Mole said. The skin crinkled at his temples; his eyes were always half-closed. He coughed a lot; he had a grating, deep-sounding cough that made Mole nervous. Though Mole's concern for Llan increased, his visits became shorter. Which seemed almost as well, for the healing master insisted that what Llan needed most was rest.

As a result, Mole found himself trudging through the rain to Ranath Thrine to groom Wildfoal or to take a quartersticking match with anybody who was available. He generally matched with Ellari, Berrian's just younger brother who, in spite of being a prince, was rather a decent quartersticker. Mole's visits to Ranath Thrine, however, were often made bitter by the appearance of Prince Berrian and the river guard on their way to or from the fields where they drilled in preparation for their winter vigil. Although Berrian mocked Mole with no more than a high smile, Mole's thoughts were sharp. What was the good of readying Wildfoal or sharpening his sword skills if he was to stay at Ranath Thrine all winter?

All of this made Mole more thoughtful than usual. But he didn't brood. He merely continued—like the rain. And then after some days, the rain at last ceased, in favor of snow.

Mole spent the morning the rain stopped at the castle stables, but when he returned to his room just before noon, he found Fflad waiting for him by the fire, sitting crosslegged not with his harp but with a burlap bundle in his lap and a grin on his face.

Mole's gaze alternated between the two.

"I thought you'd never come back," Fflad said, motioning for Mole to sit down. "Knowing you, you *would* be gone the day Arien came by. And knowing Arien, she wouldn't stay until you got back—"

"Arien?" Mole spoke the name as if it were forbidden. "Arien was here, asking for me?"

"Who else would she ask for?" Fflad suppressed a grin. "I wish she'd been in the mood to wait for you! But she said to tell you hello for her. And to give you this." Fflad hefted the burlap bundle toward Mole.

Stepping back, Mole asked, "Is it really for me?"

"Of course it's for you! And if you don't hurry up and open it, I'll open it myself. I'm dying of curiosity. You've no idea how hard it's been for me not to take a peek inside—"

"It's a present?"

"Yes," Fflad said. "Yes, Arien did mention something about that. Yes, it is a present, indeed. A birthday present."

"But it isn't my birthday." Mole scratched his head.

"We don't know when your birthday is," Fflad said. "To-day might be your birthday as well as any other. Now open it. I want to see the look on your face."

"You know what it is?"

Fflad shrugged. "Yes. And no. Arien told me she was going to make you a present a long time ago—last summer, I think. But she's done such a good job of keeping the thing secret that I'm not sure what it is, even though she's been working on it in all her spare time."

Mole's smile faded. "In all her spare time?"

Fflad's brows stiffened. His eyes dulled to match Mole's. "Well, I can't say whether or not she's spent *all* her spare time on it. But she's been working at the Tutory late into the night. Mole? You look as if you've been struck by lightning! I don't know what's wrong with you, but I do know that if you don't open this now I'm going to get very impatient!"

Biting his lip, Mole took the package from Fflad. He avoided Fflad's eyes and turned the gift in his fingers, watching the shadows dot back and forth across the coarse burlap.

The object weighed oddly against his hands as he loosened the binding cords and parted the folds of cloth.

Fflad rose to his knees and helped draw the cloth away.

Mole sighed as the burlap fell to the floor.

He had never seen a more beautiful cloak. Sewn of the softest doeskin and backed with uncarded wool, it reached from his throat to the heels of his boots. At its bottom hem and at its collar the leather flamed with intricate embroidery, leafy designs patterned painstakingly in gold and green.

Mole scarcely heard his own words. "It's fit for a prince."

Fflad's eyes widened. "The greatest prince could wear it with honor. This is no small bit of work. To embroider cloth takes hours, but to push a needle through doeskin . . ."

Blinking uncontrollably, Mole nodded.

"Well," Fflad prompted. "Won't you try it on?"

Cautiously Mole swung the cloak over his shoulders and draped it over his arms. He had no looking glass, but he could imagine how he looked; he could see the sweep of the cape from his shoulders. He could feel firm warmth couching his arms. He could smell faintly the aroma of the skins. It fit him so snugly, so thoroughly, that his posture straightened and his chin extended itself. But heavy on his shoulders was a grim realization. "Arien," he murmured. "Arien knew my cloak was threadbare. She knew there was nothing I needed more than a new cape—"

"Arien has a way of knowing things like that," Fflad broke in. He sighed and took a seat on his bed. "Arien told me you'd like it. And I think you do like it. But I wouldn't be able to tell by looking at your face."

Mole only stared, blankly. "Where is Arien now?"

"She told me twice," Fflad answered, "that she'd be at the Tutory."

With a swift nod Mole strode toward the door. The doeskin cloak lapped at his heels.

A blast of wind met him at the courtyard door. The edge of the blast made the cloak sway against his knees and cling to his breast; the smell of snow was in the air. A storm was marching in from the north.

"Arien!" he cried, not caring how the wind scattered his words for all Avy-Ellarwch to hear. "Arien!" The only answer came from the thrashing limbs of the tree, from the hum of the wind across the surface of the courtyard fountain. Mole dashed across the flagstones to the Tutory steps, clutching at his throat and staring at the shuttered windows above.

He seized the latch. But before he could shove his way through, the door opened. On the threshold stood Arien.

For a moment she stared at him, cheeks drawn, eyes wide. Then, without warning, she dashed to him, closed her arms around his neck. It was some time before Mole realized his arms were clasped behind her back. He lifted her from the stairs, kissed her cheek, and placed her on her feet, again.

Tears began when she looked at him. "Mole!"

His anguish drained away. He brought a hand to her chin and silenced her. "Arien. I'm sorry. I was wrong—"

"But Mole—" His finger crept up to graze her bottom lip.

"You don't have to say anything. This whole misunderstanding has been my fault. All of it. I was just jealous—"

"Mole!"

For the first time Mole realized that her face was white with horror; the fury with which she gripped his elbow was something more turbulent than love.

"What is it?" Mole asked, suddenly cold.

Arien's eyes filled with tears and she bit her knuckle.

"Arien!" Mole demanded. "What is it?"

"Mole! Mole!" she sobbed. "Mole, it's Llan!"

"Llan? What about him? Arien." He shook her.

"He's dead! Mole, he's dead!"

The words circled the rim of Mole's mind then drove blades of pain into every limb. His grip on Arien loosened, then his hands fell to his side. The voice of the wind chattered in his ear. Wraithlike clouds billowed over the roofs. He could taste nothing but the promise of snow. Then he felt his arm arching around Arien, supporting her as they went through the doors into the warmth inside.

"The masters told me," Mole said softly, "that he died without pain. It was something like—something very much like falling asleep, something as painless, as natural, as quiet as falling asleep."

Fflad's eyes mirrored the flames in the grate. He shivered a little, as if a slice of frigid air had reached him through the shutters. "But he won't wake up. We won't see him again. I . . . I can't believe it."

Mole's eyes swept past Arien to fix on Orne, who had curled up in a black cape next to the hearth. His face was fired with all the colors of the blaze behind him; the lights moved and danced across his forehead, making the dullness of his eyes unreadable.

Edging nearer Mole, Arien looked at the fire, then at the shutters. "This room is bigger than it used to be," she said. "You could stable Wildfoal here and still have room enough for all your cots."

Silence followed her remark.

"There are only four of us now," Fflad stated. "Only three living in this room."

Orne shifted closer to the fire.

Shivering again, Fflad brought his knees up and clasped his arms around them. "I don't understand it! It doesn't make sense! All from a little fall from an apple tree, Llan gets sick. Then, just when he seems to be doing better, something goes wrong that the masters can't explain, and—"

"It wasn't simply the fall." Mole studied Orne's face, which had grown sadder at the mention of the accident. "The masters told us from the very beginning that it was much more than that—a deeper sickness."

"But it started with the fall!" Orne turned toward the fire. "When I took him into the rain, it didn't help his cough—"

"It won't help to blame ourselves." Arien's voice was almost sharp. She pushed her fingers into Mole's palm. "Would-haves won't bring Llan back. We've already buried him. We ought to bury our sorrow as swiftly. The sooner we rid ourselves of the sadness about Llan's death, the sooner we'll begin to remember the pleasant things, as we now remember only the pleasant things about Rhawn."

Fflad sighed. He gazed back into his memory. "Like the time Llan listened to five of my ballads at one sitting."

A faint smile brushed across Mole's lips. "Or the time Llan told me that a goblin was hiding in the peach orchard, and we both stomped around under the trees all evening, me with the Sword."

"Or how Llan always used to repeat those stories about being bitten by a wolfman or a biviper—"

A moan from Orne interrupted Arien. "How can you talk like that?" he said. "How can you talk about how Llan was when he isn't finding goblins anymore! Instead he's lying in the earth by the river. All because I pushed him out of the tree!"

Arien flew to her feet. "Orne!"

"It's true!" Orne bunched up in his cloak.

When Arien shot a glance at him, Mole rose to his feet. "It isn't your fault, Orne, and you know it. Don't be foolish."

Turning to Mole, Arien said, "I think I'd better go, Mole. All our dispositions will be better in the morning."

After Arien had gone, Mole put out the candles while Fflad secured a second bar over the shutters. None of them spoke, and the sounds around them—the sputtering fire, the scouring wind—seemed loud in the emptiness of the room.

Once the room was dark, except for the glow of the fire, Mole moved to Orne and urged him to his cot. "Come, Orne," Mole said. "Cheer up. It will all seem better in the morning."

Stubborn silence followed. Then, as Mole worked to tuck the blanket around the foot of the cot, Orne said in a thin voice, "Mole?"

"What is it?"

"Mole, where's Llan now? I mean, we buried him under the trees by the river. But where is he? Where's the *real* Llan."

Mole felt helpless. "I don't know. But the poets, who have been right before, have said that the dead all go to live in a place of beauty called the Other World, where they live forever with the Emperor."

A pause.

"Then where does the Emperor live?"

Fflad's voice answered, remote from the shadows beside the storm-rattled shutters. "The Emperor lives in the north, the far north, far beyond all the northern mountains, where north itself ends. So the poets have said. But you mustn't worry about Llan, Orne. Though he has been taken from our circle, he's in good hands. You ought to worry about yourself."

Although Orne did not answer, Mole thought he heard him

whisper the word *north* to himself. Whatever, he seemed more quiet, so Mole crept across the floor to his own bed.

But sleep did not come quickly, and when it did it was filled with uneasy visions and sudden wakings. Painted on the blackness Mole saw first Llan, then Arien, then great white mountains rising in the north. He churned in his blankets, battling notions that dived at him from the dark. He heard the storm, the fire, the sound of breathing from Fflad and Orne. He heard voices calling in his memory. He saw the glint of the Sword against the wall and felt the firm wood of the ash staff at his bedside. He remembered his oath of the staff and wondered whether Llan's death was something he could have prevented, whether it was a punishment for some misdeed of his own.

· 4 ·

Beyond the Orchards

MOLE awoke to dawn sifting through the cracks in the shutters. The fire had long since sunk to white ashes on the hearth. "Go to sleep," he told himself; it was early yet. He pulled himself back into his blankets. But morning persisted in coming through the shutters, and Mole's blanket was thin. He soon sat up, pushed the tangles of hair from his eyes, and looked around the room. Fflad was only a black shape beneath the window. And in the dimness, Mole fancied that Orne's cot was vacant.

He stared, then squinted, but the picture remained. Orne's blankets spilled from the edges of his empty cot.

Mole swung his feet to the floor. "Fflad!" His whisper hissed in the frozen silence.

Fflad stirred slightly.

"Fflad!" Mole repeated, fumbling for his boots and clothes. He pushed them on and donned the doeskin cloak before Fflad moved again.

When Mole reached him, he shook the boy's shoulder.

"Oh Mole," Fflad moaned. "What do you want?"

"Orne's gone. He's not on his cot!"

Fflad's eyelids crinkled, and his fists burrowed under him

when Mole snatched his bedclothes aside. But at last he lifted his head and opened one eye at Mole. "So he's gone. So what? He's probably down at the river, by Llan's grave. You can't blame him."

Mole considered. "He might be. But he might have gone someplace else, someplace more dangerous."

Fflad pushed himself partway up. "Where?"

"Anywhere. You know how upset he was. You remember the time Rhawn died, when Orne ran away into the mountain caves. I think he's doing the same thing now, running away. He wants Llan back. Maybe . . . maybe he's gone back to Misty Mountain."

Fflad rolled to his feet. "In that case, we've got to overtake him before he gets too far. If he goes south into the mountains, he may meet goblins."

"He may meet goblins in any direction." Mole moved to Orne's cot, where he placed a hand on the canvas near the blankets. "He hasn't been gone long—it's still warm. If we hurry, we can catch him."

They reached the courtyard while Fflad was still fastening the brooch on his cloak.

"We ought to check Llan's grave," Fflad said.

"And perhaps the Tutory as well," Mole added. He scanned the dark walls until his eyes caught a grey shape in the shadows of the eaves. "Orne!" he shouted. His voice rang. "Orne, if that's you, come here. Now!"

The shadows shifted.

From the pocket of darkness, clad in a traveling cape with the hood drawn around her ears, came Arien.

She didn't bother to greet them. "Orne *is* gone, then?" she asked.

"He's gone," Fflad said. He arched an eyebrow. "You know about it? Have you seen him? He was upset—did he come to you for comfort?"

She shook her head, then paused. "But let me tell you why I'm here. I couldn't sleep last night. I lay in bed until the storm ended, just before dawn. By that time I couldn't stand Enna's snoring any longer. So I went to the window for some air. The moon had just set. It was so dark I couldn't see anything, but I heard footsteps on the ice down in the courtyard."

"Orne?" Mole guessed.

"I don't know. But I started having a feeling, an awful feeling like the ones I used to have when you went on your mountain trips, Mole. I sensed that Orne, upset as he was last night, had left Avy-Ellarwch. So I dressed and went to the Tutory—I almost went to your chamber, but I didn't want to wake you until I was certain Orne had gone. I stayed at the Tutory long enough to find out that someone had taken a supply of cheese and apples from the pantry—"

"That doesn't have to mean Orne's planning a journey," Fflad interrupted, kicking at a bit of ice with his foot. "Even the masters borrow cheese once in a while. Orne might not have been the one who took it. And he may only have gone as far as Llan's grave."

"I'm not that dense, Fflad," Arien resumed impatiently. "I thought the same thing, so I went to the river, but no one was there. And no one had been there. I looked in the trees and called for Orne, but I couldn't find him. He simply wasn't there."

Mole scratched at his jaw and looked at the gate. "Then we can have no notion of how far Orne intends to go. He may have set out for Misty Mountain. He may have fled into the hills to be alone. He may want to reach the sea. But in any case he is in danger; safety ends beyond the orchards these days. We must go after him. And quickly!"

"Not so fast," Arien said. "We'll lose ourselves if we simply rush off. We have no idea how long it will take to find Orne. We need food."

"And Mole ought to bring the Sword," Fflad put in. "I dare say it won't do us any good to find Orne if he's facing a band of goblins and we're undefended!"

"Mole must bring the ash staff along as well," Arien added. "It may serve us as more than a walking stick."

Swiftly Mole nodded. "We should take horses, too."

"Not horses," said Fflad. "We won't be able to follow Orne's trail, wherever it leads, on horseback. We'll have to go on foot. And we'll have to have a tracker—"

"I can track," Mole said, "a little."

"A 'little' tracking," Arien stated, "could end us all up in a cavern or bog. Fflad's right. We need a person who can follow trails, someone who has had experience.''

Fflad suggested, ''I know someone who knows trailcraft.
Last summer, when some of us got lost on a hunting trip, he
brought us back to Avy-Ellarwch by backtracking the trail
we'd just made.''

Arien's eyes brightened. ''Who is it?''

Fflad glanced sidelong at Mole before responding quietly,
''Prince Berrian.''

Mole blanched. ''Berrian's quite out of the question.''

''Why?'' Arien demanded. ''I don't see why!''

''He just won't do it, that's all,'' Mole said, backing away.
''Berrian would never agree to a mad chase like this, dashing
off so early in the morning.''

''I don't see why he wouldn't,'' Arien retorted. Beneath her
cloak she placed her hands on her hips. ''But I think I see why
you wouldn't want him to. You're still jealous. Even now.''

A prickling in Mole's cheeks stifled his answer.

''Oooh!'' Arien's eyes were slits of blue. ''Moleander Ammarbane! You infuriate me! Who do you care about more,
yourself or Orne? Is it such a bitter thing to fetch Prince Berrian and bear his company for a day or so? By the Emperor,
I'd ask him to come myself, but I doubt if it'd be proper for
me to barge into the royal bedchambers!''

''Others can track as well as Berrian,'' Mole returned, ''and
some better, I'll bet. *I'll* not go after him!''

Fflad forced himself between Arien and Mole. ''Now let's
not allow this to get out of hand. Our concern is Orne; with
every word we speak he takes another step away from Avy-
Ellarwch. Mole, please be reasonable. Don't set your jaw like
that. Arien, I'll go to Ranath Thrine myself, if you'll gather
some food for us—''

''I doubt,'' Mole said, his eyes smoldering at Fflad, ''that
Arien's dear Prince Berrian will agree to come.''

Arien turned crimson and spun around. ''Fflad,'' she said,
''tell Prince Berrian that *I* wish him to come. Immediately.
He's gentleman enough that he'll oblige you.''

After a long glance at Mole, Fflad nodded and left.

With a scowl at the morning sky, Mole strode toward the
boys' quarters. Reaching his room, he lifted the Sword from
its bracket and strapped it around his waist. The scabbard

rested well against his knees, and the familiar touch of the cold hilt against his ribs eased his tautness.

Next Mole found the ash staff. Oddly, the polished wood of the rod felt colder in his palms than had the steel of the Sword; somehow he could not bear to grip the staff for very long, so he propped it between his knees when he flung himself onto the chair beside his writing table.

"Are you going to pen a love poem?" the Sword quipped.

Ignoring the weapon, Mole doused the feather quill in the inkpot, groped for a sheet of parchment in the dimness, then began to scrawl a hurried message. When he had finished, he could not be sure that what he had written could be read by anyone else.

He reached the door before he realized he had left the staff leaning against the chair.

"Bother!" he growled as he snatched it up. "Bother this whole morning. Bother this adventure! If it is an adventure, indeed!"

He found the others by the gate. Prince Berrian had joined them. The prince, however, seemed flustered; his velvet tunic bunched oddly about his belt, his hair was tangled except for where his fingers had passed through it, and his cloak sagged from one shoulder. Though he was beaming at Arien as Mole rounded the great tree, he glowered when he saw Mole.

Mole halted and measured Berrian with a cold stare.

But Berrian only grinned and closed his hands together. "Look who's just come. By Hwyl, I'd no idea there were so many in our company. With the whole orphanage along, I doubt we'll catch up with that runaway for a week." He faced Arien. "As happy as I am to track for you, know this: I can't be away from Ranath Thrine very long. My father needs me, for I am crown prince." His eyes flickered toward Mole. "And in only a few days, when the snow comes, I must ride with the river guard."

"Highborn wretch!" Mole muttered under his breath.

"Furthermore," Berrian went on, "we need to tell my father where we are going. Because I am my father's heir, he is always concerned about me. Should he find me missing without reason, he might suppose me to be carried off by hawk riders or goblins—"

Mole coughed. "We don't want your father to worry, Prince Berrian. But we've no time to wake him up and explain everything to him. I've left a note; that should be enough. Now, stop your talk and find Orne's trail."

For a moment Berrian faced Mole, eyes aflame. But he tossed his cloak over his shoulder and knelt to examine the muddy earth near the gate. "These must be the prints of your friend," he said presently. He traced an ice-feathered mark in the mud. "It's fairly fresh, and it was made by a smaller person." Berrian stared first at the print, then at the northern hills toward which the toe pointed, then back at the mark again. "The left boot has a cleft in the heel," he noted to himself, "and at the beginning, at least, he started northward." Berrian lifted his head. "Your friend left just before dawn."

"We know that already," Mole said, folding his arms. "Get on with it."

Berrian tossed his head; after a warning glare at Mole, he moved northward along the hill, sweeping the grass with his eyes, halting every few paces to stoop and touch the frost-whitened earth. Arien followed him at once, hoisting a sack over her shoulder. She shot a glance at Mole.

With Fflad beside him, Mole came after brandishing the ash staff in his fist. When he watched the mist settle over the northern hills, cold and rigid, he could not prevent a shiver.

"I didn't think Orne would go north," he told Fflad. "Mon Ceth is south. The sea is east. What could he find in the north?"

Fflad replied with a shrug. "I don't know what he *wants* to find, but I do know what he *will* find if he goes far enough—a nasty bog and an even nastier set of cliffs." They walked in silence until Fflad spoke again. "I don't suppose you have my harp tucked away in that cloak of yours?"

Mole shook his head.

Fflad smiled swiftly. "I really didn't expect you to, but I thought I'd ask anyway." He sighed. "If I were sensible, I'd know that this trek will be too short for any harping. But I have a strange feeling that we may be gone for a very long time indeed, that I may want to put my fingers to a harp before we're through."

Mole started to reply, but a drop of water on his forehead silenced him. For they had descended the hill of Ranath Thrine and moved in beneath the hemlocks at the edge of the forest. Avy-Ellarwch sank behind them.

The morning vapors receded as the sun came over the mountains. But the day remained damp and cold. The clearings between the trees were black, ready for snow. In the quiet bareness, Orne's prints appeared now again in the soft, leaf-padded earth. This forest, so near Ranath Thrine, was certainly more dark than dangerous; all the same, Mole felt prickles of apprehension, an undefinable restlessness, not helped by Berrian's slow tracking.

Before noon the trees gave way to ragged stretches of heath. Orne's trail wound its way across ice-crisped meadows to follow a barren ridge above the River Thrine.

When the sun stood as high as it would go, Berrian called for a halt. Mole, impatient to be on, almost suggested that the rest of them stop while Berrian forged on ahead. But he held both his tongue and his temper.

"Are we getting closer to Orne?" Arien, red-cheeked with cold, flung the food sack to the ground near her feet.

Prince Berrian bit the end of his finger before answering. "I can't tell for certain. If we're any nearer, we're not very much, for his tracks aren't any fresher—"

"Thanks to your blasted tracking," Mole said. "If you could follow a trail faster than a hen can walk, we'd have overtaken him by now. Bother tracking, I say. If I only had Wildfoal, I could ride ahead and find Orne in an hour."

"I doubt," Berrian replied coolly, "if that beast of yours could catch up with anything." He smiled. "Besides, you can't follow a trail on horseback—everyone knows that. I suggest you be patient. If you can."

Mole's fingers twisted around the ash staff.

"Come now," Arien broke in, glancing between them, "we didn't stop to bicker. We stopped to eat." She thrust her arm into the bag and produced a handful of apples. She passed them hastily to Mole and Berrian, though she remembered Fflad only when she pulled wedges of cheese from her pack.

They ate in silence, under the swirling sky.

Before they finished their meal, Berrian, who had been watching the brown ribbon of river, broke the hush. "I'll be seeing more of this wild country, I think. If you look between those two rocky hills, Arien, you'll see the edge of the Thrine-fens, where the River Thrine finds its beginnings. Between the fens and Ranath Thrine is where my river patrol will ride."

"*Your* river patrol?" Mole scoffed, squeezing a bit of bread in his hands. "What, do you lead it? Or was it your idea?"

"Was it *yours?*" Berrian retorted.

Mole flew to his feet, but before he could speak, Arien reached out in front of him.

"Look, everyone!" she exclaimed. "Look! It's a flower."

By the time Mole looked down, Arien had already taken, from somewhere near his feet, a bright green, small-leaved plant crowned with tiny golden bells, blossoms that twitched slightly although no breeze blew. When Arien cupped the plant in her hands, the flowers seemed to glow faintly against the palms of her hands.

"Emperor!" Fflad gasped. "A flower? Here?"

"Alive, in this frost?" Berrian bent nearer.

Forgetting his anger, Mole dropped to one knee.

Arien held up the flower for all of them to see. The blossoms seemed to scatter stars of saffron light on her face. "Such a thing on the edge of winter . . ." Her voice trailed off. "It's beautiful . . . so lovely. Does anybody know what kind of flower it is?"

"I've no idea," Berrian said.

"Nor do I," Fflad said. "I've seen nothing like it."

Mole grappled with his memory. "I know," he said at last, and Arien looked at him. "Or at least I think I know. I remembered seeing frozen plants like this on Mon Ceth. It's your namesake, Arien, the mountain-flower. It's an arien."

While Mole spoke, Arien, eyes on the flower, brought from her cloak the book Rhawn had given her. By some trick of the light, the white binding seemed as golden as the blossoms of the arien. She pushed the book open. When she spoke, her voice did not seem to be her own. "This book holds two poems," she murmured. "At first I could understand neither.

I read one in Gwarthan's tower, but I think—now—that I need no wizard to help me understand the other.'' Arien's eyes fell to the book in her lap.

"Of Garren's daughters, Amreth shall claim three,
　　One of valley, one of fell, and one of tree;
　　One queen of light, one queen of flood, one queen
　　　　of briar,
　　One sought by love, one taught by scorn, one
　　　　wrought by fire.

　　One shall lift her husband's sun
　　With magic from an aeddenon.

　　One shall fell enchantment find
　　The gates to Vivrandon to bind.

　　But Fellflood's angry oath shall break
　　For a wilted blossom's sake.

　　And when wars and warlocks all are gone
　　Will Amreth's daughters seek the dawn.''

Mole seized Arien's shoulder as she finished. "If you want my opinion, this poem isn't hard to understand. It's easy enough—even Fflad will agree with me. It's a prophecy about the three women Amreth will choose to make powerful enchantresses.''

"According to legend,'' Fflad added, reflectively, "two have already been chosen, Cara, the wife of High King Llarandil, and Rhea, Lady Fellflood, wife of Fifran II of Vivrandon. I've read poems that describe the wonders they worked with their magic, which, it is said, came from certain flowers. But both of them have been dead now for many years, unless it is true, as some chronicles say, that those chosen by Amreth are immortal . . .''

"Two have lived their magic,'' Arien mused, turning the flower in her hands. "But one remains to be chosen.''

Mole cleared his throat. "Legends and old stories about enchanters and prophets! You can't get away from them, even here." Mole avoided Fflad's eyes. "I say we stop telling stories and start walking. Orne—"

"But what about the flower?" Fflad protested. "I mean, flowers don't just spring up by themselves at this time of year—"

Berrian's fingers knotted his hair. "Moleander is right, for once," he said. He regarded the arien warily. "We've wasted enough time."

Fflad's objection was cut short by a gesture from Mole.

Though the others stood in a tight circle, exchanging glances, Arien remained seated, even when Mole offered her his arm. Instead of rising, she stared at something Mole could not perceive, a few paces in front of her. She brought the flower to her lips and touched the topmost blossom against her nose. Mole thought he saw yellow sparks on her fingers where they had touched the arien. He seemed to mark the growth of a glow, sallow at first but then almost crimson, on Arien's cheeks and in her eyes.

"Arien?" Mole said. Her wrist was hot to his touch.

"Arien!" Berrian crouched in front of her and put quivering fingers to her cheek. Arien started; turning her eyes away she dropped the arien into the pages of her book, pressed it closed, and slipped it back into her cloak.

"Let me help you up."

Mole bit the end of his tongue as Berrian lifted Arien to her feet.

As they started along the hill again, Arien dropped away from Berrian and walked with Fflad. Her head bent, her arms together in front of her, she spoke to no one. But now and then Mole saw her lips twitch.

"It's enchantment, my boy," said the Sword. "I seem to recall your saying that magic was part of adventure, but it seems that you're not enjoying the enchantment *or* the adventure very much."

But Mole hardly heard what the Sword said.

The course of the afternoon brought them from the highlands downward, toward a broad lowland shrouded in fog. This Berrian identified as the Thrinefens. Clouds rolled above the rocky declines dotted with wind-bent rowans and frost-blighted alders; a wind screamed across the higher rocks, casting a deep cold through Mole in spite of his cloak. But to Mole, worse than the cold, worse than the fens spreading before them, worse than fleeting visions of Orne among wolves, was the sight of Arien's troubled frown.

At nightfall, Mole argued with Berrian on the last long slope before the lowlands. Berrian admitted that he had seen no clear print of Orne's foot on the stony and frozen ground of the slopes. Orne might be an hour or a day ahead of them. Yet Berrian refused to hurry into the fens before the light failed. When Mole threatened to enter the marshes by himself, Berrian declared that if Mole refused to be sensible he would return to Ranath Thrine at once. "The fens are full of meres and quicksand and marsh wolves; they are perilous by day but deadly at night." Berrian's eyes smoldered. "I have placed the crown prince in too much danger already."

Only when Arien told Mole not to be rash did he agree to wait until morning. But he brooded while Arien distributed a cold supper. After they ate, they spread their cloaks on the cold ground, and for a long time Mole lay shivering, listening to the sounds from the fens below; the mist hissing in the trees, the slosh of distant swamp things in the meres, the splinter of ice under the weight of invisible feet. He thought he heard the far-off cry of something in the fens that could have been either a wolf or a hawk.

"I don't see why Orne wanted to go to the Thrinefens," he muttered. "It doesn't make sense. It doesn't make any sense at all."

• 5 •

Over the Frozen Gate

To Mole's relief, Berrian's tracking seemed swifter in the fens,
for Orne's footprints were plain in the damp sand. Even Mole
spotted signs—now smudged, distorted, and filled with brack-
ish water—of Orne's passing. Yet he was restless. Danger
seemed to lurk everywhere: behind the tattered draperies of
moss and in the ranks of dry weeds that rattled at the edge of
the morning breeze. Bits of mist hovered like wraiths rising
from the soaked soil. Great heavy trees wreathed the edge of
the marshes. Then as they pressed on, the trees gave way to a
vast mud flat, thick with shoulder-high reeds. Here Orne's
trail was hard to find, and the going was painfully slow. Tiny
green lizards darted between Mole's feet, hissing and clicking;
burrs lodged themselves in his cloak. The air thickened.

But soon the reeds began to thin as they veered westward. In
the region they entered, everything seemed pale; the mud was
greyish-pink, the life grey-green. Now they were truly in the
marsh.

The smell of the swamp, choking even near its margins,
grew unbearable. Pockets of stagnant water filmed with

frozen slime produced an odd kind of mist that rose and twined like thread.

The morning passed with no sign of Orne or of the end of the swamp. Mole followed Berrian in a half-trance, dodging mechanically stands of grass or meres of greenish water. The sun continued to shine, but it warmed the cold marshland very little. Now and then Mole's numb grip on the ash staff would loosen, and he would have to wrestle the mud for it.

Great mud basins and black-rimmed pools increased in size as they went on, now at a snail's pace, for they were obliged to follow a chain of tussocky mounds that wound its way through the peat and steaming meres. Mole awoke enough to watch his footing. He knew an erring step could throw any of them into a swallowing pit of quicksand. He took Arien's arm and watched the water-spattered prints of Berrian ahead of him.

"This is wretched," Arien growled. "There isn't any ground left. We'll soon sink. I only hope that Orne didn't—"

"Worry about us, not about Orne," Berrian said through his teeth. "The boy's feet are lighter than ours, and he passed here last night when the mud was frozen."

"Last night!" Mole exclaimed. "I knew we should have followed him last night. Can't you hurry, Berrian?"

Berrian strained to pull a leg from the mud. "Hurry? In this? Are you mad? If we hurry, we'll all be killed!"

"If we don't, Orne will!"

"I think," Berrian retorted, "that the four of us, one of us a prince, are more important than a silly little boy!"

In a flash of rage, Mole lunged toward Berrian.

But he lost his footing. One leg sank into mud. He cried out as he felt himself falling. He grasped at the nearest reeds but missed. The mud sucked him to his calves. Arien reached for him, but her fingers closed short of his, and the water swallowed him to his waist.

Berrian pushed Arien aside. "Your staff!" he shouted. "Push your staff to me, quickly!"

Straining against the mud, Mole obeyed. But there was a gap between the staff and Berrian's fingers. Mole stretched. He struggled with the mud. And in a last desperate effort, he hurled the staff forward, holding to it with outstretched arms. Berrian caught the staff, and with a single heave of his powerful shoulders dragged Mole to solid ground. The mud moaned behind; it slavered and gurgled in its defeat.

Mole stood shivering as the others pressed in around him. Fflad and Arien, when they had steadied him, began to scrape the mud from his boots, tunic, and cloak.

"That was too close," Fflad said. "Thank the Emperor for Prince Berrian's presence of mind!"

Berrian, a few paces away, rubbed his shoulder thoughtfully. His cheeks were bright with exertion, but his eyes remained cold. He regarded Mole as if he were an overpampered child rescued from a rainstorm. When he saw that Mole was looking at him, he brushed the dust from his sleeves. "If you wanted to fight me," he said, "you should have waited until we reached safe ground."

Flushing, Mole held himself rigid. "I've paid for my anger, Prince Berrian." He looked at Berrian, eyes keen. "And, though it pains me to say it, I thank you for your help. You saved my life."

Berrian blanched for a moment, then the color returned to his face. "I am a prince," he said. "I would have done the same for less than you." His chin rose perceptibly. "Can you walk?"

Mole swallowed, then nodded.

Berrian masked a half-smile, pivoted, and began to pick his way onward. Fflad patted Mole, and the three of them set off after Berrian.

The remainder of the day seemed uneventful to Mole. He hardly noticed when Berrian stumbled into shallow mud and scrambled up, muttering. The cliffs of Fellheath began to climb above the horizon of mist, but Mole felt confident they would find Orne in the marsh.

Twice Berrian lost the trail and found it again. Once Arien sighted wolves on a forested mound; Mole unsheathed the Sword until the hillock sank into the vapor behind. Mole heard often, as they moved to the far reaches of the marsh, the beat of wings in the clouds above. Fflad heard them, too, and looking up suggested that they were the sounds of geese that rested in the ponds of the fens. But Mole knew better. He had seen the geese gliding south over Avy-Ellarwch long before.

By late afternoon the land rose toward the cliffs. The swamp brush gave way to boulders and scattered, leafless larches. Yet still the bootprints continued, leading out of the fens toward the cliffs, until they led, quite abruptly, into a chaos of fallen leaves under a spreading larch.

Berrian stooped over the heap of leaves and began sifting through them, frowning and grunting as he worked.

"I'll bet," Mole said to Fflad as they watched, "that Orne slept here."

Fflad squinted at the sun. "If so, he's almost a day's journey ahead."

Mole reflected on the path they had taken through the fens. It seemed Orne had crossed only the neck of the swamp; his intent, then, could not be the marsh itself. But where was he bound? Mole frowned. Not half a mile north stood the first moorland cliffs, the crumbling battlements of Fellheath.

A flutter of wings stirred the fog above.

At the same time Berrian brought forth an apple core, a twisted green thread, and a cheese rind with molding leaves clinging to it. "He ate and slept here. Although I haven't checked, I'll wager he set off from here toward those cliffs, toward that cleft in the rock. He's gone up onto Fellheath. He's gone to Vivrandon!"

"But why?" Arien asked. "I don't see why. If he wanted to find memories of Llan, why didn't he go to Eber Seador or Mon Ceth? He knows the way to both, and neither road is as dangerous as the Thrinefens or Fellheath. If he simply wanted to get away from us, why didn't he go to the river, or to the woods near the castle. Fellheath? That doesn't make sense!"

"You're sure this is Orne's trail?" Fflad asked Berrian.

Berrian sighed. "What do you take me for?"

"But I don't understand," Arien persisted. "There isn't anything beyond Fellheath but mountains—mountains after mountains."

Mole froze. "I know," he said suddenly, "where Orne's gone."

"Where?"

"I don't know why I didn't think of it before. My memory is so thick."

Berrian looked on unblinkingly.

"Orne asked me when I put him to bed," Mole continued, "something about what happens to people when they die." Fflad bit his lip and nodded. "I told him about the Emperor and the Other World, and he asked me where they were. I told him that the Emperor lived in the far north, beyond Fell-heath—"

"Of course," said Fflad. "Of course."

Slumping to a seat on the tree root, Berrian grimaced. "Now's a fine time to remember. We've come all this way for nothing. We can't follow him into Vivrandon."

"Why not?"

Berrian laughed. "Why not? Must you always be so dense? Because if he's gone to Vivrandon, he's as good as dead! Didn't you hear what Gwarthan said at the council? The boy won't cover a mile before he's ridden down by hawk riders. They'll skewer him for a feast. And even, if by some miracle, he escapes the warriors of Vivrandon, he still won't survive. Wolves or starvation will get him."

"Everything you've said," Mole countered, "is good reason for our going on. We came to save him, didn't we?"

"Of course. But we didn't come to sacrifice ourselves, no matter what you say. If we go to Fellheath, we'll be no help to Orne. None at all. We can fight wolves, but we can't fight deathless riders. Besides, we've scarcely enough food to make it back to Ranath Thrine as it is. Right, Arien?"

She nodded reluctantly.

"We can't abandon Orne!" Mole said.

"I'm not suggesting we abandon him," Berrian returned. "I'm merely pointing out that we're in no position to help him. The only intelligent thing to do is to return to Ranath Thrine. There you can ask my father to raise a search party. You can follow on horseback. As I recall," Berrian added, "you've always been eager to ride on a horse and wave a sword. I don't see your objection."

"But I see yours," Mole answered. "I see why you don't want to go on. Not because turning back will help Orne, for horses can't cross the Thrinefens or climb the cliffs of Fellheath." Gripping the staff between his two hands, Mole looked at Berrian and said in a low voice, "You want to quit, Berrian. You're afraid, afraid for your own life."

"I'm afraid I don't know what you mean."

"You know exactly what I mean. You are the Crown Prince of Thrinedor. No matter who else is in danger, you can't be. You're too precious, too breakable."

Beneath his cloak Berrian's arms tightened. "You're a fool," he sneered, "a lowborn, ignorant fool. What do you know of the ways of princes? How dare you accuse *me* of cowardice? I would hang you for such words if I were king! Certainly I am careful. I don't place myself in foolish peril because I don't live only for myself, as common people do. I live for the kingdom. I *am* the kingdom." Berrian moved his head sharply toward the cliffs. "I would not be taking only Berrian to perish on the moors. I would be taking Thrinedor."

Mole wanted to shout at Berrian that he was a human being, too, but then he decided he wasn't sure he really was. And anyway before he could speak, he felt a tug at his sleeve and a voice in his ear. "Whether you're ignorant of the ways of princes or not," Arien whispered, "you're quite ignorant of the ways to *persuade* princes. We need Berrian's help, and we won't get it if you keep this up. Be quiet and leave Berrian to me!"

Arien brushed past Mole and approached Berrian. She knelt in the leaves in front of him to gaze into his face.

"If you've come to condemn me or talk me into going on," he said, turning away, "don't waste your breath. I've made up my mind. I'm going to be sensible. I'm going back to Ranath Thrine, and I don't care whether you think me a coward or not."

"I? Think you a coward?" Arien laid a hand on Berrian's knee. "If I thought you a coward, I wouldn't have asked you to come in the first place."

Berrian folded his arms. "My contract with you is finished, if that's what you're driving at. I said I'd track to the borders of Thrinedor, no farther. That was our bargain."

"It was." Arien sighed and looked down to where she

curled her hands over Berrian's knee. "I don't blame you for not wanting to go on. Fellheath *is* dangerous, and you *are* a prince, with more to think about than yourself. And above all, Orne isn't *your* friend. We're grateful, then," Arien went on in a lower voice, "for your help so far. We wish you a safe journey back over the fens."

Berrian's eyebrows curved upward. "Er . . . yes. Thank you. But certainly you don't mean that all of you are going on—into Fellheath."

"I'm going," Mole said grimly, "no matter who else will come with me."

Fflad's eyes flew between Berrian and Mole. "I'm going to Fellheath, too."

When he saw the same light in Arien's eyes that he had seen in Fflad's, Berrian took her hand from his knee and drew her up beside him on the root. "Arien," he said in a voice that Mole could scarcely hear, "certainly you don't plan to go with them, to a frozen doom on Fellheath!" His eyes searched hers. "Come back to Ranath Thrine with me. Please. Please don't be foolish—"

"I must go on," Arien said evenly. She allowed Berrian to close his hands around hers. "I don't have a choice; it's almost as if I were Orne's mother. Or at least his sister."

"But you may never find Orne. And the danger to your-self—"

"I've been in danger most of my life. I don't plan to start avoiding it now. Besides," she said, "I have Mole to protect me."

Berrian's right hand, slowly loosening from Arien's, dropped into his lap, then climbed to the pommel of his sword. "That will not provide you enough safety," Berrian murmured.

"It will have to. I won't change my mind."

Berrian sighed. "Only for a few days," he muttered.

"What was that?"

"Only for a few days," Berrian repeated, looking harried. "I'll track for you—but only for a few days."

Her face suddenly bright, Arien kissed him on the cheek. "Thank you!" she said.

"Arien," Mole said gruffly, "come pick up your pack. I dare say we'll need everything that's in it."

Although Arien obeyed, her eyes flitted back to Berrian, who, whirling in his cape, started for the far side of the leaves.

"I think," the Sword said as Mole shouldered his baldric, "that your dear Arien doesn't know as much about the ways of princes as she pretends."

Chill as the wind, a wolf's howl penetrated the fog as they gained the last rise, the level of the downs, after hours of half-climbing, half-crawling up the series of stone-littered rock faces. Always during the climb, the brow of the cliff loomed above; below, the marshes and mud flats settled in a blanket of cold vapor. The world was only the freezing cliff and the rounded forms of the other clifftops leading eastward and westward into obscurity.

At the top the Great Moor, the High Wold of Vivrandon, terrible Fellheath, opened before them, endless, patched in grey heather bent by the steaming winds. Rags of cloud hurried across the darkening sky like restless ghosts. Mole looked on, astounded, for no tree broke the emptiness. How the people of Vivrandon survived here Mole could not tell, but he was certain they must be hardy.

"You'll need luck to catch Orne here," the Sword said. "Only wolves and hawk riders do much catching on Fell-heath!"

"Orne can't be too far away," Arien said, though it looked as if the moor went on forever.

"Fellheath is wide but not endless," Berrian said. "It ends in the north at the Mon Lluwall, the Secret Mountains. The clouds hide them now, but the Mon Lluwall are twice the height of the Mon Dau and as wild as the Mon Evann of the west."

Mole strained his eyes but could see no hint of mountains beyond the clouds. And though the wind had cleared the near reaches of the heath, Mole could see no sign of Orne.

Before long night was upon them. Nothing else changed; Fellheath stretched on, flat, frozen, unbroken. And from somewhere near them came howls that were not wind; wolves followed them. Mole thought he saw a shape thread the mist behind them, but in the increasing dimness, he could not be sure. He fingered the Sword as he walked.

Berrian discovered a swale in the plain to which they brought weeds to make beds. They ate sparingly and silently.

Perhaps, Mole thought, Berrian would desert them that night.

The others curled into their cloaks, but although Mole was numb from the wind, he did not try to sleep. He wrapped the doeskin cloak around his shoulders and positioned himself on the lip of the hollow against a few ice-crusted boulders. He watched, waiting. For he knew that he heard wolves near at hand.

At first it was so dark he could barely make out the nearest sleeper, but as the night wore on, the wind began to die. An opening in the roof of cloud revealed a pale triangle of midnight sky studded with a single bright star, a star that seemed to brighten the entire hollow. Yet too soon the clouds drifted over the star, and dark closed again over the moors.

In spite of his resolution to remain on guard, Mole heard wolves only in his dreams before dawn.

Mole's first glimpse of the morning would have given him more pleasure if he had had something in his stomach. The day was clear and calm, but stingingly cold. Mole awakened to a thin frost on his cloak, and he was glad enough to rise and warm his blood.

He shivered beside Berrian, who gazed toward the low blue line of mountains crisp against the sky. Mole thought he could see flecks of snow on the mountain crowns.

He asked Arien about their supply of food. She replied, somewhat tartly, that their supplies were her affair, not Mole's, and she distributed a few bits of cheese before they set off. Berrian took the lead almost without glancing at the ground; Mole suspected that he had lost the trail altogether. But he said nothing.

Because Arien and Fflad had agreed to carry the food sack between them, Mole was obliged to bring up the rear by himself. At least this allowed him to keep an eye on Berrian.

They heard no wolves.

Midday brought a scanty meal. Berrian gobbled half his share and tucked the rest in a pocket. Mole noted this with a glare and resolved to keep watch again that night.

Feeling hollow, he once more asked Arien about the food.

"If you want more, you won't get it from me," she said. "I've given you all I have for now. If you're still hungry, watch the moor. And good luck. I haven't seen a living thing on this fell except the wolves."

"I've seen hawks," Fflad said dully, "twice. But I doubt they'd be worth trying to eat."

"Hawks?" Mole echoed, suddenly alert.

Fflad nodded.

"That means," Mole said, "we're moving nearer the heart of Vivrandon. Where hawks fly, hawk lords ride behind. If we're not careful, we'll come face-to-face with a power as evil as Ammar's. But the power here is more deadly. Goblins can be slain, but the riders of Vivrandon are deathless. From what Gwarthan told me, I doubt that even the Sword could strip aside their armor of enchantment."

Berrian thrust a reproachful look at Mole. "If the hawk riders are invincible foes, why do we continue to go deeper into their territory? It's madness! It was madness to come here in the first place. And the madness grows every moment we remain here. How do we know that the warriors of Vivrandon haven't already fed your Orne to their falcons?"

"If we find him slain," Mole fired back, "we will return to Thrinedor."

"If we find him slain," Berrian stormed, "we may find ourselves caught between armed patrols. I won't die for foolishness, Moleander. I won't perish in this wasteland for your friend!" He drew his sword and extended it toward Mole. Mole could see reflections of smeared clouds on the silver. "Go on if you wish." Berrian turned his head away from Arien. "All of you. But by Hwyl I will return to Ranath Thrine. Now."

Mole shoved the blade aside. "Go if you want, and may the wolves feed on your corpse when you tumble from the Vivrandon cliffs. Go! We have no need for a coward's sword. Nor have we need of a tracker who looks at the earth only to polish his royal boots!"

"You think I've lost the trail. I wish I had, for then I might be able to turn the more sensible of you from this doomed search. But I've not lost the trail, and indeed, even on this rocky heath I've not had to search to find it, for your friend's prints have been joined by those of another."

Fflad bolted to his feet. "Has he been captured?"

"If so," Berrian replied, "his captor is a dwarf, for the new prints are little bigger than Orne's own."

"Gwarthan?" Mole hazarded.

"I doubt it," Berrian said. "Gwarthan is in Ranath Sharicom."

"Then who has joined him?"

"Whoever it is," Arien said, "is wiser in the ways of this heath than we are. Haven't you wondered why the four of us together, nearly full grown, haven't overtaken Orne? Why, we've been continually falling farther behind?"

Though Berrian lowered his sword, he did not sheath it. "Which is why all of you are mad to keep on. If Orne's new companion is as capable as he seems, we've no chance of catching up to them. The gap will only widen. And, if you're still worried about Orne's well-being, he's in better hands than ours right now."

For the first time a doubt shadowed Mole's mind. He wanted to answer Berrian, but he could think of nothing to say. Berrian's logic seemed flawless. And Berrian, looking on with a grin of triumph, knew it. "Now then," he said briskly, "we ought to get started for Thrinedor. It's a long walk."

Mole, feeling hollow inside, did not answer.

Fflad heaved a sigh and nodded at Berrian.

"I knew you'd all see things my way—eventually." Berrian sheathed his sword, tossed his cloak over one shoulder, and started away from them in a southerly direction.

An outcry from Arien halted him. "Wait!"

He raised an eyebrow at her.

"You can't go back to Thrinedor," she said. "None of us can."

"Why not?"

Arien turned the color of frost. And when all eyes were on her, she dragged the food sack into her lap. Under Berrian's stare she bunched it, lifted it, then tilted it to the earth in front of her. A few bread-crumb-dusted rocks spilled out.

"It was madness for me not to tell you," she said with a dull frown, "but a few minutes ago, we finished the last of the food."

· 6 ·
Fellfire

THE sky burned saffron above the ashen stretch of the moor. As the sun sank toward the horizon, touches of gold alighted like birds on frozen shafts of heather. Silence spread with the shadows across the heath.

Eyes fixed on the southern emptiness, Mole cupped his hands over the top of the ash staff. He propped it against the inside of his knee as he squatted to survey the distance.

"Bother Berrian! Blast it, I should have gone with him. I shouldn't have let him go alone. He's been gone so long. I wouldn't be surprised if he's forgotten about finding food altogether—"

"I doubt if his stomach will let him forget," Arien said. She lay in her cloak, her hair spilling over the boulder behind her back. The sunset glinted in her eyes as she said, "Berrian agreed to find food for us. When he does, he'll come back. Just trust him."

"Trust him? How can I trust him. Didn't you think it odd that our fragile crown prince would be the one to volunteer to find food? The only food on Fellheath is in the backpacks of Vivrandon warriors. Why was Berrian so anxious to go for food when he's always so concerned for his own safety?"

"Perhaps," Fflad suggested, "because staying here to guard us isn't much safer." Cross-legged in a patch of dead grass, Fflad wrinkled his nose at the horizon. "A hawk rider might appear at any moment."

"Still, Berrian wanted badly to be the one to go."

"Berrian wanted badly to be the one to go," Arien stated, "because *you* wanted so badly to be the one to go. You know that."

Mole frowned and pretended not to hear Arien. "I think he saw his chance to desert us."

"How can he desert us?" Arien sat up. "He doesn't have enough food to make it to Thrinedor."

"How do we know that?" Mole retorted. "He may have stored up food he didn't tell us about. In fact, only a few hours ago I saw him hide half his bread in his tunic. If he's been hoarding food every meal, he'll have enough to see him back through the Thrinefens, at least."

"When will you stop being suspicious of Berrian? He hasn't been 'hoarding' his food!"

"And how do you know that?"

"I know, because the food you saw him save has already been eaten. He gave it to me."

Mole's ears felt warm.

"All the same," he said, pushing himself to his feet, "I'd feel much better if he were here and I were out hunting food." Mole began to pace along a seam of broken rock, glaring southward. Out of the corner of his eye he saw Arien sit back again against her boulder.

In a moment Fflad said, "I'm glad you're here, Mole, if it makes you feel any better. It's reassuring to know you and the Sword will stand between Arien and me and whatever happens to wander along this moor. It wouldn't be the same if Berrian were here. I've seen you kill goblins and sorcerers, but I doubt if Berrian's fine jeweled sword has been out of its scabbard more than twice."

Although he didn't turn around, Mole began to pace more slowly.

"You see," Fflad went on, "I've felt a kind of *dread* all day. It started when we first saw the mountains." Fflad dropped a weed he had been twisting in his fingers and pointed toward the north. "Do you see that tall peak, the nearer one? I can't be sure, but I think it's Mon Cathyn, the mountain where Sir Rheidol met the Hardanog dragons. Maybe I've read the ballad of Sir Rheidol too often, but a line from Cyranus's poem keeps whispering through my head." Fflad paused, then recited in a voice like the crackle of leaves rolling in an autumn wind, " 'To die a death foretold by dreams, from welcome lands away—' "

Mole spun around. "I'm sure there are more pleasant lines of that poem," he said. "Think of another verse."

Swallowing visibly, Fflad nodded. "I'll try."

"Good." Mole swung around and began pacing again, but before he could take three steps, he heard a murmur, like ice water over stones, of Fflad chanting in a very low voice:

> "Water, mountain, star of fire under velvet grim
>   and black
>   The dragons of Mount Cathyn lurk on beyond
>   the frozen track."

As Fflad sang, Mole noticed that Pinegar, the brightest star of the north, had appeared in the dimming mist over the mountains.

> "Fairest of the High King's sons, Prince Rheidol
>   from the sea
>   Comes with gold to battle terror, Vivrandon to
>   free.
>   Over harshness, over frost, over the moorland's
>   frozen gate
>   The brooding mountains rise like specters where
>   the dragons wait."

After a pause, Fflad went on:

> "Ne'er to return, ne'er to feel warmth, ever
>   doomed to stray,
>   To die a death foretold by dreams from wel-
>   come lands away."

Mole winced. "Fflad! I know you've memorized more cheerful poems."

"Indeed. But I find it hard to think of them."

"I suggest," Mole said tautly, "that you force your mind to brighter things. If that doesn't work, take your dagger out and practice with it. You may need to use it while I'm gone."

Fflad leaped to his feet. "While you're gone?"

Arien joined him. "You can't leave us!"

"I have to," Mole said, stomping his foot. "I'll go mad if I stay here, and we'll all starve if we can't get something to eat —soon. I must go find some food. And Berrian, too. Preferably both."

"A lot of good food will be if you find us dead!" Arien stormed. "Fflad has only that dagger Berrian gave him. And I have nothing at all!"

"Your tongue could kill a wolf," Mole returned drily. "You're in no real danger if you keep low until it gets dark —no rider will spot you. In fact, when I return I'll be hard-pressed to find you, even when I know where you are."

"What about wolves?" Fflad asked. "They won't need to see us to find us."

"That's what your knife's for!"

Fflad paled. He cast a sidelong glance at Arien, but although she read his concern, she looked still at Mole.

"If you must go," she said fiercely, "go now and be quick about it. And see," she added, "that you and Berrian don't get into a swordfight in the middle of an enemy camp!"

Ignoring Arien, Mole whirled and stalked over the brow of rocks. After he took a dozen steps, he looked back to see that Fflad and Arien were standing to watch his retreat.

"Get down!" he shouted back to them. "It isn't dark yet!"

But it was nearly so, he observed before he went much farther. Shadow cast a mist over the earth so that his steps were often false. Still he loped at an even pace. He had seen which way Berrian had gone and the point at which he had disappeared on the horizon, and he kept the place in his vision until he reached it, then continued on in the same direction. Only his hunger hindered his swiftness; his legs buckled against rocks, and twice heather snatched the ash staff from his hand.

Soon he saw lights. He would have thought them to be low

stars were it not for their color, which even at a distance seemed red.

He proceeded with more caution, and when he was close enough to see the movement of shadows in the ovals of fire, he hunched and stole catlike along a low copse until he dropped behind a jutting rock. Since Berrian had come this way, Mole reasoned, he must have found the source of these lights, too.

Torches. Mole soon identified them, more by the smell of tar on the wind than by their look, for he was distant yet. Sliding past the rock, he scurried to the cover of a wind-bent currant bush.

From this vantage point he saw that the torches, four of them, were affixed to spears at intervals along the moor. Between them were campfires, and around them men crouching over the flames. Mole saw a few men in the shadows stretched out on rocks, but he saw no horses, so he assumed this to be a camp of footsoldiers. When one of the two sentries stepped into the light of the torch, Mole noted other details. The men wore heavy armor. Their cloaks and tunics, unless it was a trick of the light, were grey and black with crimson borders. The colors of Vivrandon. The sentry fitted a black-plumed helmet to his head while Mole watched. The other guard wore on one shoulder a burlap pad that Mole recognized as the protection falconers wore.

Hawks. Mole searched the dim sky but saw nothing more than stars.

He had come to find food and Berrian, not hawks. He swept the camp with his eyes. Footmen bound across Fellheath would need provisions. And without pack-horses, supplies would have to be carried in backpacks. Within the circle of torches, packs would be cumbersome; certainly the warriors had piled them elsewhere.

Mole soon discerned a torch set apart from the others. In its glow stood a watchman with his back to Mole, and on the ground were shapes, oblong shapes, that might be packs.

Although Berrian might be among the packs, Mole thought of food. It would be a simple task, he judged, to creep to the outpost and slip something out of a pack or two. The prospect was exciting; it would take daring, cunning, and a little luck.

"Here's your adventure," the Sword whispered.

Mole smiled slightly. "I know."

He edged from his cover. Crawling half on his belly, he inched along the rocks just beyond the margin of firelight. As if the glint of his teeth or eyes might betray him, he welded his lips together and made slits of his eyes. His hands ached from the frost, but he crept patiently along, ears alert.

Twice he kicked stones; the first clicked aside, but the second rattled hollowly down an incline. Mole froze. Grey eyes from the nearest torch swung toward him; he saw them probing the darkness, keen like the eyes of falcons. Only blackness saved him from their gaze.

Stars blazed on the horizon by the time Mole reached the first pack. Glancing back toward the camp, Mole saw that most of the warriors were chanting something near their campfire. The nearest watcher leaned against his torchstave, dozing.

Mole took bread from two packs before he saw the shadow.

After tucking his loot into his tunic, he stilled.

The shadow, as was Mole, was busy with a pack. Hunched a few yards away, it was silhouetted oddly against the fire of the stars. Though Mole had noticed him, he was heedless of Mole.

Berrian? In the refracted light of the torch, Mole could not tell. But he could make out bunched shoulders, a lock of hair loose, and a sweep of a cape.

Lowering his hand to the Sword, Mole whispered, "Berrian!"

The man's head snapped around.

A little louder. "Berrian!"

The man rose to his haunches. His face struck starlight. To his horror, Mole saw not the face of the Thrinedor prince but the features of a man he had never seen before. Torchlight gleamed red on the man's brooch, which bore the silver image of a hawk.

"Who's there?" demanded a voice, matched by silhouette lips. "Who's there!"

Springing to his feet, Mole bolted away. A shout went up behind. He fled on into the dark. From the corner of his eye he saw the camp rouse to life. He saw the shimmer of a dozen turning helmets, a dozen rising swords. A torch pole leaped to the hand of a watchman. Shouts rushed toward Mole like a wind. His own breath hissed in his nostrils, hot with fear, swift with exertion.

Blindly he ran, pushing into the cloak of night. The flame of torches and armor sparkling gathered on the black horizon behind him. The warriors followed.

Yet, once he was back in the dark of the heath, Mole's panic ebbed. His senses, scattered by astonishment, returned. Running would not save him from his mistake, he realized. Not by itself. He must be cunning, or the Vivrandon warriors, by the simple virtue of their numbers, would capture him.

A glance at the sky told him he was running north. North. Toward Fflad and Arien. Possibly Berrian. But he could not now alter the direction of his flight. Behind him the torches parted; two of them beaconed on his right and one on his left. Mole chilled at the realization that he could save Arien and Fflad only by finding them before a hawk warrior did.

So he concentrated on the terrain and on speed. He groped in his memory for details, pictures to match with the blurred knots of stone, the ghost branches of bushes, and the shadowed tracts of grass. He veered westward as he ran.

He choked down bits of bread between breaths, for his hunger made his strength flag. By the time he finished the first crust, he was approaching a familiar backbone of crumbling rock.

"Arien! Fflad!" he wheezed. He scarcely slowed even though he saw shadows lifting in front of him. "Get up! Get your things! There are hawkmen—warriors—coming from the south."

A shape reared out of blackness. "Mole?" It was Berrian's voice. "Mole! What have you done? Have you brought that war camp down on us?"

Mole pitched to a blind halt. "Yes! They're coming! Now don't waste time. Are Arien and Fflad here?"

Replies peppered the darkness, but soon Arien's voice rose above Fflad's. "Blast you, Mole! I told you not to go! I knew something like this would happen! Berrian came back only a few minutes after you left!"

"I must have missed you," Berrian interjected. "I returned from a war camp in a ravine east of here to avoid running into any riders—"

"If you just hadn't been so idiotically impatient!"

"Lash at me all you want," Mole barked, "but do it while we're running. They're coming, I tell you!"

Like stars in twilight, torches appeared on the horizon.

"Come on!" Mole urged, sensing confusion around him. "Those aren't figments of your imagination. And there are warriors coming with them. Now, do you all have the strength to run?"

"We've eaten a little," Berrian answered in a low voice.

"I suggest, then," Mole snapped, "that we fly!"

By dawn they stumbled along at scarcely a walking pace. Mole limped, pain from his legs molding his face into a protracted wince. Beside him Fflad shuffled, arms clinging to his chest, his cheeks puffed with effort. Berrian, at Mole's other flank, strode doggedly, but his ankles turned on stones, his knees buckled at intervals, and his head hung in front of him so that wind-ruffled bangs hid his eyes. Linked to his far arm was Arien, whose steps trailed behind. In her weariness, her head pressed against Berrian's shoulder, her arms twined around his sleeve like ivy. His cloak half-covered her.

As much as Arien's preoccupation with Berrian irked him, Mole said nothing. He could not waste the strength. And he knew that words would be useless after what he had done.

Sorrow for his rashness was as keen as the smart in his lungs.

When the sun balanced on the eastern horizon, they spoke.

"Can't we stop soon?" Arien moaned. "We've been running all night, and my feet will fall off if we go much farther." She pulled herself up on Berrian's arm. "Certainly the warriors won't follow us this far. Surely they've turned back. They must have. I've seen nothing of their torches since midnight."

"We've got to press on nevertheless," Mole said. "We must be sure we're out of their reach before we halt. I'm afraid that Berrian and I with our swords and Fflad with his knife would be a poor match for them."

"Yes," said Berrian, "we've got to keep running. Only when we're safe should we rest."

"But when will we be safe?" Fflad inquired.

Berrian lifted his head. "Soon. I smell a river in the north wind. If there is a river near, it will be the great river of Fellheath, the Fellflood, which flows southwest from the mountains to join the Ystadun in the Great Forest. When we cross the Fellflood, we'll enter the high reaches of Vivrandon called the Fell Downs. There we'll be safe; the warriors won't cross the river."

"Why not?"

"The part of Vivrandon north of Fellflood Vale is more wild than Fellheath. Goblins live there, it is said; the only men who survive there are sorcerers or outlaws."

"*That's* where we're going to be safe?"

No one bothered to answer Arien's question.

They continued on in silence through the morning. A few clouds lifted and hovered in the west, but the moorland stretched on with no sign of Berrian's river. Sniffing the wind, Mole smelled something more like smoke than river water.

They stopped at noon long enough to eat, then pressed on. Although Arien refused to speak to Mole, she did let him help her, along with Berrian. She slept more than walked that afternoon, but as fatigued as he was, Mole carried her along. Whenever he began to slump in his hold, he found Berrian watching him, stalking on remorselessly. Mole would counter then by throwing his head back and stretching his legs to match Berrian's strides.

The afternoon warmed only a little. Clouds remained high, silver and cold. Twice Mole spotted hawks wheeling in the west, black specks under the clouds. And once, unless it was a trick of his eyes, he saw a bird soaring in the north; it was unlike the others he had seen, for though it had the wingbeat of a hawk, it did not seem to be earth or soot colored, but the color of frost.

Toward evening Mole saw horsemen. They were bound toward the sunset, away from them, so he said nothing. All the same he was glad to see night set in; he knew they were approaching well-used trails just south of Fellflood Vale, and night could make them invisible there.

Mole saw the river late in the day.

They came on it unexpectedly. One moment the fell seemed as unending as ever; the next it dropped away at their feet in terraced clay cliffs, punctuated with flat rocks. Below them, in a narrow coomb, moved a dusk-colored river. Beyond the river another bastion of cliffs climbed into a distance of rounded earthen hills, which faded into the jagged northern mountains.

"This must be Fellflood," Berrian said when they had descended to the flats. The earth was so soft that Mole's boots sank almost to the heel. "Fellflood Vale is notoriously muddy this far north. But these river bottoms are very fertile near Rathvidrian. At least they used to be. When I was small, my father bought almost all our potatoes and wheat from the Fellflood Vale farmers."

Mole found it hard to believe that anything could grow in such cold mud as this, even farther downstream. Rathvidrian was there, he knew. And that too gave him a feeling of cold. He could feel the presence of the fortress, even here. He imagined the rock towers lifting from the black river. He could see in his mind torches glittering from battlements onto the river's face like fireflies. Shuddering a little, he looked eastward into the advancing gloom of evening. Upriver he followed the turns of the Fellflood until it vanished, pinched between two bluffs. It seemed to him that a glow capped the cliffs, as feeble as candlelight, beyond the hills.

"Look!" he breathed. He pointed for the others to see.

Dusk made the lights upriver more bright.

"Rathvidrian?" Fflad said.

Berrian shook his head. "We're too far north and too far east. Rather I think that it's an old Vivrandon trading city called Fellhaven."

"I'll bet it's a muddy place to live," Arien remarked, looking at her toes.

Mole nodded. He thought he could see more lights on the heath south of the town. "Yes. I've heard of Fellhaven. Ellari was talking about it the day after the council. He said that at last report Fellhaven had declared itself separated from Prince Ichodred and Rathvidrian, that it was an outpost for the decent folk of Vivrandon. Ellari and I were going to suggest to King Ellarwy that we use Fellhaven as a stronghold for our invasion of Vivrandon next spring, but—"

"What does Ellari know?" Berrian broke in. "Use Fellhaven as a stronghold? Utterly foolish. My father's already thought of that and rejected the idea. Although Fellhaven is commanded by an enemy of Ichodred, Daerwyn Fellflood, the town is no more than a dozen stick houses surrounded by mud and pickets. It would hardly be sufficient for military purposes—"

"Military purposes?" Mole burst out, steadying himself with the ash staff. "Who's worried about military purposes *now?* I'm talking about *our* purposes!"

Arien brightened. "Yes," she said. "We ought to go there at once."

"I doubt if we could walk that far tonight," Berrian said sourly.

"Besides, how do we know Fellhaven is still in friendly hands?" Fflad said. "How do we know that this Daerwyn person hasn't been overthrown by a group like the one that chased us?"

"We can worry about Fellhaven tomorrow," Mole sighed. "We can worry about everything tomorrow. The main thing now is to cross the river so we can get a proper night's rest."

They all looked at the Fellflood. Its murky water twined past them, masked in deepening shadow. Unlike the River Thrine, the Fellflood seemed to make no sound. It moved past them mutely.

"I'm not sure that's the main thing at all," Arien said, glancing at Fflad. "I don't think I'm up to crossing."

"How deep is it?" Fflad asked, returning her look. "I mean, if it's much over our boottops, we'll freeze tonight from getting wet."

"Yes." Arien sneezed.

"If we sleep in this mud," Mole said, "we'll sink all the way under before morning."

"We can't go back to the heath," Berrian added.

"It looks as if," the Sword piped, "you've caught yourselves between a rock and a muddy place, so to speak."

"*You've* been no help," Arien snapped. "I haven't heard *your* suggestion."

"That's because," the Sword replied crisply, "I haven't given one."

Arien threw up her hands. "I can't stand this anymore."

She glared at Mole. "Whatever we're going to do, let's do it quickly."

"We've got to cross the river," he said.

Berrian glowered but nodded.

So they moved to the riverbank.

Mole unbuckled his swordbelt as they neared the river. Berrian unfastened not only his sword but also his baldric and cloak; these the prince rolled together and collected in his arms.

"I'll carry the food sack for you," Mole said to Arien as they reached the silt-strewn edge of the river.

"No thank you. If I drown, I want the pleasure of knowing the rest of you will miss me at least for my provisions!"

Mole shrugged and surveyed the river. "This seems as good a place to ford as anywhere else. But let's be careful."

He coupled the Sword and the staff in his hands and lifted them above his head. Glancing back at the others, he stepped into the mud near the bank, then moved slowly into the river. The water first encircled his ankles. A moment later it gripped his shins just below the knee. He felt the bottom of his doeskin cloak brush the surface of the river; he wished he had thought to tie it up, but he hadn't, and it was too late to regret his error. Though the river scarcely moved, its water seemed thick, like flowing mud, as it pushed against his boots, threatening to make him topple. And it was so dark he could scarcely make out the earth-colored ripples around him.

Looking back he saw the others following. Arien was nearest, holding her sack in front of her at arm's length, face intent on the black water. Fflad and Berrian tottered after her; Berrian's belongings balanced across his neck.

As soon as Mole turned toward the far shore again, he heard a splash. Arien screamed. Mole hooked the Sword under his arm and spun around in the same moment. He lunged and almost before he realized what was happening, he caught Arien in his arms as she pitched toward the water. The current dragged at their legs. Pushing against the mud, Mole heaved upward, drawing Arien back to her feet.

Ashen, Arien looked up at him as he urged her toward the far shore, and she began to shake before they reached the riverbank. Mole let the Sword and staff clatter to the sand, but

Arien pushed away from him. She began to cry. "Mole. The river—Mole."

The others splashed to the bank. "You're safe now," Mole said. "Your legs are wet. There's no more harm than that."

Arien pressed her fists to her cheeks. "It isn't me! By the Emperor, I'm not worried about me. It's the sack. I . . . I slipped and let go of it. And it fell into the water."

Mole's eyes shot to the river, but he saw only the Fellflood's blackness, glossy like the night sky above.

"Don't you understand? I've lost it. I've lost our food! Mole!" She came nearer. "I called you a fool for not heeding my advice on the heath. But I didn't heed yours a few minutes ago. I took the food sack across myself. And now I've lost all our provisions—"

"It won't help to be upset," Mole said smoothly. He glanced at Berrian, who folded his arms and turned away. "I have a feeling we'll miss that sack. But Arien! It could be worse—"

"Yes, it could be," said the Sword from the sand. "You could have been carrying me."

Mole pushed the Sword in farther with his toe. "It could have been worse," he repeated. "We could have been deep in the wilderness. But as it is, we can arrange for food at Fellhaven if we go there tomorrow. In the meantime," he added, flattening a hand against his stomach, "we're too tired to be hungry anyway. At least I am."

They climbed up only the first hill to sleep. Berrian and Fflad threw themselves to the ground immediately. Arien seated herself against the hillside and shivered in her coat while Mole looked back over the river, which now mirrored the rising moon.

"How wet are you?" he asked her.

"To my thighs."

Mole arched his back. "Here, then," he said, shedding his cloak. "Wear this for the night."

"But what about you, Mole? You'll freeze."

"You'll freeze, if you don't have extra warmth." Without turning around, he let the cloak down on her knees. "Anyway, it isn't as cold here, so near the river. Nothing's frozen. We're out of the wind now, off that bothersome moor."

"Mole?" Her voice was quiet.

He turned around and looked at her.

Her eyes flickered up at him. "Thank you."

"Don't mention it," he answered with a wry grin. "You might make me realize what I've done." He left her to sleep on the far side of a bush, mostly because he didn't want her to see him pull his arms into his tunic.

When at last he slept, he dreamed he was lying in the warm glow of the greatest of bonfires.

• 7 •

Maddwn's Gift

DAWN arrived with a rumble like the music of trumpets. Mole woke with a start and leaped up. A mountain of thunder-clouds had formed; there would be rain. Or snow.

The others soon awakened.

"I had an awful dream," Fflad said. "It was almost as if I had read one of Cyranus's death poems right before I went to bed and dreamed of it all night." He paused, gazing at Mole with unsteady eyes and went on. "I dreamed that the moon had turned all the sagebrush the color of bones. I remember hearing the river sigh nearby. I saw a shape flit overhead, partly hidden by branches. It flew over twice, so I soon saw it was a hawk."

Arien handed the doeskin cloak gently to Mole. "That doesn't sound like such a terrible dream."

"That's not the worst of it," Fflad answered. "The hawk wasn't the ordinary kind, though they're bad enough in this country. It was white, as if it were the ghost of a hawk."

Mole bent nearer. "I thought I saw a white hawk. Yester-day. But it wasn't in a dream."

"I'm not sure," Fflad said darkly, "that mine was, either."

"Enough prattle about dreams and white birds," Berrian

said. He brushed the breast of his tunic with delicate fingers. "If you've sense enough to put your cloak on, Mole, we'll start for Fellhaven."

Mole flung the cloak over his shoulders. "Fellhaven? Are we bound for Fellhaven just like that?"

Berrian regarded Mole wearily and said, "Where else are we to go? Rathvidrian? What else can we do? The only sensible thing is to arrange for supplies at Fellhaven—perhaps an escort as well, if this Daerwyn person wants to keep on good terms with my father. Then we'll go back to Thrinedor in haste—"

"Because your father's worried about you," Mole finished, scornfully. "He'll be fretting about his tender crown prince!"

Berrian's cheeks flashed with color. "He'll be fretting about you, too, as you'd know if you had a brain in your head. He'll be worried about all of us. Knave! Whatever you wrote in that note can't have told him we'd come as far as Fellflood. He'll send out search parties—"

Mole threw his arms across his chest. "That isn't the point! The point is about going to Fellhaven. We can't just blunder to the gates. We've got to find out if Ichodred's hawk riders have captured it. I suggest that all of you wait here while I go have a quiet look around."

"A quiet look around?" Berrian sneered. "The last time you took a 'quiet look around' you brought a hundred warriors down on us. No. You won't go again."

"Then you go."

Berrian cast a glance toward the river. "It won't do any good."

"Are you afraid to go?"

"By Hwyl no! But listen to what I'm saying! All of this spying won't do any good. It'll only waste our strength. Remember, we don't have any food. Whoever controls Fellhaven, we've got to go there. To be Ichodred's captives would be better than to starve to death here."

Arien nodded slowly. "I think he's right, Mole."

Scowling, Mole brushed his hair aside. "Oh, I know he's right. It's just—"

Fflad placed a hand on Mole's shoulder. "Orne?"

Berrian threw up his hands. "After all that's happened to

us, you're still worried about Orne? You must be mad, Moleander! Yes, mad. Even if we had the strength to follow him, we couldn't. We've lost his trail."

"I'm not mad." Mole lifted the ash staff, then sunk it heavily in the mud. "Don't blame me for my regret about Orne. I haven't suggested that we try to find his trail."

"Then you agree that we should go to Fellhaven?"

"I told you already that you were right."

Berrian blinked. "Oh. Very well then. Let's not waste time."

They traveled along the riverbank in single file with Berrian in the lead. Though the sun was screened by whisps of cloud, it felt warm to Mole as he trudged along. It made the bands of ice on the hillside bushes glitter; the face of the river, however, remained clouded and sooty.

Morning waned. At intervals Mole glimpsed distant pickets lifting out of the river or from gorges in the clay cliffs above it. He held the Sword's hilt when he thought of hawk riders. And he felt an odd sting in his eyes when he thought about Orne.

The only really annoying thing about the walk, though, was the mud. Although they kept to the very edge of the hills, far from the river, the earth beneath their feet became increasingly softer, taking the prints of their boots more crisply at every step. Mole looked down in order to watch the mud caking on his heels; doing this he almost collided with Berrian, who halted in front of him without warning.

Berrian motioned for the others to keep back but pointed to the ground. There, leading up from the river and disappearing into a ravine between the hills, were two sets of small footprints.

Mole recognized at once the notched bootprint. "Orne."

Although Berrian looked away, upriver, he nodded.

"Orne?" Arien said in disbelief. Then, "How fresh are the prints?"

"They were made last night," Berrian replied.

"Then Orne and his friend," Mole said, squinting up the ravine, "are less than half a day away from us."

"Not very far," Berrian returned, "but far enough."

Mole looked at Berrian. "We've got to follow him. Now. We're closer to him than we've been since he first left Avy-

Ellarwch; we've got to catch him now or give him up forever—''

"We don't have any food," Arien protested. "We need to
go to Fellhaven for supplies. Then we can follow him."

"If we go to Fellhaven, Orne will be out of our reach."
Mole appealed to Arien and Berrian alternately. "Besides, we
don't even know if we can get food at Fellhaven; we may be
taken prisoner, if Ichodred controls the village. We must
follow Orne now!"

"Now," Berrian repeated quietly. He sighed. "You are
right, Moleander."

"Don't you see?" Mole went on fiercely. "It's the only
way. No excuses about hunger or princeship will do. If we
don't go after Orne now, he'll be lost to us forever!"

Berrian's cheeks tightened; he said, coolly, "Are you deaf,
Moleander? I said you were right. We ought to track your
friend."

Mole blinked. "You agree?"

Berrian stiffened. "You said I was right this morning," he
said awkwardly. "One admission deserves another. But," he
added with a flush of red when he saw Arien watching him,
"we'd better find your Orne soon and hope he has some food
with him."

Mole could not subdue a grin as Berrian started into the
ravine.

Their progress was rapid, for the trail was plain enough
even to Mole. It led almost directly northward, winding along
the ravines between the downs. The hills held a hush beneath
the quiet morning sun. But they held cold as well; a brisk
breeze began to blow out of the north from the direction of the
Mon Lluwall, which stood out jaggedly against the sky. During the walk Mole's attention flitted between the prints on the
earth and the looming shape of the nearest mountain. Orne, it
seemed, was heading straight toward Mon Cathyn.

Not far from the Fellflood, they came on a gorge between
two hills. A few sparse hemlocks clustered in the gorge deeps;
in the shadows of their branches rested a pair of applecores in
a chaos of footprints. Berrian was eager to press on, but Mole
lingered long enough to snatch up something from the base of
the thickest hemlock. He held the object for the others to see.

"A feather?" Fflad questioned.

"A white feather. And a big one." Mole turned it in his fingers.

"From your white hawk?" Arien said. "Do you think this hawk has something to do with Orne or his companion?"

Berrian glared at the feather. "Maybe it's a bit of down from the lining of Orne's coat," he said. "Enough about feathers. Let's go on."

Although Berrian insisted that they were gaining on Orne, the prints in the muddy places seemed little fresher. Mole watched with concern as the mountains closed in. Already a great chain of peaks soared to the east, crowned with timber and clouds. And in the north Mon Cathyn swelled, separating itself from its sister mountains as they walked. Mon Cathyn seemed both darker and taller than the rest; its slopes looked sheer, weather-beaten, ice-shingled. In spite of himself, Mole kept thinking of Sir Rheidol.

Afternoon came. Streaks of cloud barred the sun; it began to be colder still.

Then, without notice, Berrian stopped.

He straightened, frowned, and sniffed the air.

"What is it?" Mole demanded.

"Can't you smell it?"

"I can smell something," Fflad said, "but it smells like frozen mud."

"No." Raising her chin, Arien sniffed. "No. I smell it, too. It smells like . . . like smoke . . . a fire . . . but with something cooking on it."

"Mutton," Berrian said. "Mutton."

Mole drew a deep breath. "I can't smell anything—" He cut himself short. "Wait. I do *see* something. Look. Over that egg-shaped hill. Isn't it smoke?"

And soon each of the others saw a grey thread of smoke coiling into the blue from beyond a humped ridge.

"I detest mutton under normal circumstances," Fflad said, fingering his collar. "But I dare say I'd like it now."

Mole noticed that each of them had already taken involuntary steps toward the hill. "No one cooking meat here will want to share it with us. Remember, even the hawk riders avoid these downs. Only ruffians live here. And goblins—"

"Men or goblins, I'd eat with them." Arien licked her lips.

"If goblins had you in for dinner," the Sword returned, "that's just what would happen. They'd have you for dinner."

"Who says they're goblins?" Berrian said. "For all we know they may be a search party from Thrinedor. The least we can do is investigate."

They took little time in climbing the ridge.

Berrian and Mole reached the hill crest at the same time, then dropped down behind a thicket and waited for Fflad and Arien to scramble up behind. Mole motioned the others to silence, then lifted his head cautiously.

"What is it?" Arien whispered from beneath.

Mole motioned for silence.

Nettles obscured his view, but he made out with difficulty a cramped triangular valley below. A spot of flame there seemed surrounded by half a dozen shapes.

"What's down there?" Arien persisted.

"I can't tell," Berrian said, peering over Mole's shoulder. "But whoever it is has horses—four—no five—of them. And I don't think they're goblins; they're too big."

"If they're not goblins, what are we waiting for?"

"They're wearing skins and homespun," Mole said. "That means they can't be from Thrinedor. But they're not hawk riders, either."

"They might be outlaws," Fflad put in.

"We're outlaws, too, in a sense," Arien said. "And we're just as desperate as any outlaw in these downs. What are we waiting for? They've got food. Let's go down and ask them for some."

Though Mole hesitated, Berrian stood up. "I for one am willing to take a chance for a strip of mutton. I'm going down to meet these men, whoever they are." He glared at Mole. "If the rest of you want to say here, that's your business."

But Mole matched Berrian's strides down the hill, and Arien and Fflad kept almost to their heels. Mole walked with one hand on the hilt of the Sword, the other on the staff, and his eyes on the men around the fire, who, as Mole and his companions approached, stood up and reached for their belts but made no move nearer.

"I'm sure these men are outlaws," Mole heard Fflad mutter to Arien. "And fierce outlaws by the look of them. I almost wish they were goblins."

Mole kept a steady eye on the men by the fire; he and his companions were committed, now, beyond turning back; he could only hope for the best. He halted a dozen paces away from the nearest outlaw, halfway between the fire and the horses.

As if preparing to speak, Berrian cleared his throat. But he said nothing.

The wind stirred the flames of the campfire and ruffled the shoulders of the outlaws' bearskin jackets.

Mole felt eyes turning to him. He fumbled for words. When words came, he wished he had not said them. "I am Mole-ander of Ranath Thrine. I and my companions are traveling northward—"

The nearest man, a thickset brute with eyebrows as hairy as his jacket, rounded the fire. He began an ugly laugh, then spit onto the dust in front of him. His rough-hewn face darkened, but his eyes, so deeply set that they were scarcely visible beneath his brows, fixed on Mole. "My name is Maddwn of Vivrandon, Fellrider," he answered, mocking Mole's manner of speech. "I and my companions travel in whatever direction the wind blows us." He swept an arm back toward his men. "This is where the wind has blown us. Welcome to our home, Moleander of Thrinedor."

Mole felt the sinews of his arms tighten as his thumb found the hook of the Sword's hilt. He felt the outlaws' scrutiny, and setting his teeth, he tried to return Maddwn's stare.

Maddwn, Mole saw, wore around his mud-stiff bear-skin a belt of braided hide from which hung a tarnished war horn, a blackened water pouch, and a sheathless iron knife that seemed to reach almost to his knee. Mole found his attention welded to the dagger. He soon realized the reason; Maddwn's thoughts were there, also. The outlaw's brown fingers curled around the hilt, pressed against the pommel, and followed slowly the curve of the blade.

"We mean no harm here," Mole said. His eyes shifted to the fire, to a black rib of meat in the flames. "We want no more from you than a little food, for we are starving."

Maddwn grinned. "You want food, eh? Not surprising. Every beast in the Fell Downs moans with hunger since Prince Ichodred stripped the land of its herds." Maddwn shot a glance at one of his men, who began to move around the fire. Mole noticed another outlaw closing in behind them. "My band has eaten nothing but hawk meat and leather for many weeks." He indicated the meat with a sweep of his hand. "Now we have only this side of mutton—no more than that. If you want to eat with us, you'll have to pay."

"We have no money if that's what you mean," Mole said.

Maddwn laughed gratingly. "I didn't think you would. But there are other ways of paying. You must have something of value." Seeing the Sword glittering in Maddwn's eyes, Mole took a step back.

"I've nothing to give them," Arien whispered, "unless you think they'd like the embroidery thread in my pocket."

Mole shook his head.

"Even if I *had* something valuable," Berrian said, "I wouldn't want these brutes to have it."

"I could give them my cloak," Fflad offered.

"What? Then freeze to death on a full stomach?" Mole returned. "It's good of you to offer, but I don't think your cloak's what they have in mind."

Looking up, Mole addressed Maddwn in a louder voice. "We have nothing to trade. If you're a better man than the Ichodred you condemn, give us food. If you're not," he added, glimpsing an outlaw near the horses, "let us go in peace."

Maddwn spat again, then rubbed the dirt with his boot heel. "Your demands are unreasonable considering there are four of you and five of us, all better fighters. You might reconsider your stand."

"We certainly shall not!" Color flaring in his cheeks, Berrian stepped forward. "Maddwn," he growled, "I warn you not to do anything rash, nothing you'll regret. Give us some food at once or let us go!"

Maddwn sized up Berrian. "Such rage," he said. "Such brash words from a stripling!"

"Stripling?" In spite of Mole's swift glance, Berrian moved forward, drunk with anger. "How dare you use such a name on me? If you knew who I was, you'd not dare speak to me like that! Take that scowl from your face! Beware! For I am Berrian, Crown Prince of Thrinedor. My father is the most powerful king in the north! If you value your life, give us food and let us go!''

"But this isn't Thrinedor," Maddwn pointed out darkly.

Berrian flinched but returned, "I am my father's heir. Should anything happen to me, his riders would hunt you down and drag you back to Thrinedor to be hung from the highest oak in the kingdom. Filthy ruffian! Beware the wrath of my father!''

Maddwn ignored the fire in Berrian's eyes. He fondled his dagger. "Yes, princeling. I see that your father would do much to keep you from harm." His tongue flicked over his lips. "Much." Then, without warning, he seized Berrian's arm, plucked the dagger from his belt, and spun Berrian around, pulling Berrian's head to his own shoulder. Berrian struggled until the knife flashed into sight.

Mole's hand shot to the Sword, but he did not draw, for the other outlaws, circling in, placed their hands to their belts also.

Maddwn's eyes crossed Mole's. "Keep your weapon sheathed," he warned, edging the dagger against Berrian's throat. "A moment ago you wanted to bargain for food. You claimed you had nothing of worth. But you were mistaken. Now, let us bargain. You are free to go now, to take with you all the food you want—the mutton on the fire, the bread in our saddlebags—whatever you please. In return you will leave with us your crow-mouthed princeling. His ransom will more than make up for any losses of our mutton. It is an excellent bargain, especially because you have no choice about it. And it is so good for all of us. We rid you of this troublesome princeling, who no doubt frays your nerves with his high prattle. You, you are able to go on your way, free and fed—''

"Do you expect us to *sell* our friend?" Arien burst out from behind Mole.

"I expect nothing. I demand." Maddwn waved his dagger at his men. "And as I have said, you have little choice."

Mole tensed and slowly reached down, keeping his eyes on Maddwn. But just as his fingertips brushed against the hilt of the Sword, his arms relaxed. He examined Berrian, then smiled. "Hm." He glanced back at Arien and Fflad. "I don't see that Maddwn Fellrider has made us such a bad proposition," he said with a shrug. "He's right. We don't have a choice. We need food, and they need Prince Berrian. Besides, I'll be the first to admit that Berrian has been a pain to have with us all along. Good riddance, I say."

White crept into Berrian's cheeks.

"Mole! You can't be serious!"

"We can't sell Berrian no matter how hungry we are."

Mole lifted an eyebrow. "Can't we?"

Berrian went livid. "Beast! Churl! Who do you think you are?"

"Mole," Arien protested. "Stop! Are you mad?"

"Of course, he's mad!" Berrian bellowed. "He's been mad since we left Avy-Ellarwch. By the sorcerer's fire, if I could get my hands on you, Moleander, I'd rip you apart limb by limb!"

"Are you sure you want him?" Mole curled his lip with scorn at Berrian, whose outcry had been silenced by a brush with Maddwn's dagger. "He's like a snake, full of venom! Indeed I'll sell him to you, if you still want him."

"Mole!" Arien cried. "Mole! *Have* you gone mad? Mole!"

"I can see," Mole said, "that we won't be able to strike our bargain here." He scowled at Arien. "Have your men keep these others here, Maddwn, and you, I, and the princeling can join the horses, where I can inspect what provisions you have. If you are willing to give up enough supplies, I'll tell you a way to get twice the ransom out of this stripling prince!"

Maddwn's eyebrows fell until they almost hid his eyes. "I see you are more a man of sense than I took you for. But I don't see that we must quibble over supplies. We have much to spare."

"As they say," Mole returned, "there is honor even among thieves. If we are to strike a bargain, I must see what I will get in return for my prince." Mole smirked. "It's not that I don't trust you, Maddwn Fellrider, but I do want to see that we get provisions."

Maddwn agreed with a grunt. He called two men to stand

around Fflad and Arien, who stood pale and dazed. As
Maddwn forced Berrian toward the horses, the prince alternately pleaded with Mole and cursed him, promising him first
riches then death. When they reached the horses, Maddwn
hurled the prince to the ground. While Berrian was still
breathless from the fall, Maddwn knelt with one knee on the
prince's chest. He twirled his knife carelessly before balancing
it above Berrian's heart.

"Search as you wish," he told Mole.

Mole saw the reflection of his own smile in Maddwn's eye.

Mole rounded the steeds, browsed in their saddlebags, then
ran his hands down their tethers to the leather ring about
which all five harnesses were fastened. When he had finished
toying with the harness ring, he sauntered back to Maddwn.

The outlaw lifted his face. "Well? Are you satisfied?"

Sighing, Mole assumed a quiet smile and lifted his eyes to
the hills, where the shadows of spotty clouds roamed like
sheep.

"Satisfied?" he murmured, eyes twinkling. "By Garren,
yes!"

In a single movement Mole drew the Sword and hurtled his
boot into Maddwn's midriff. The dagger spun into the air.
Maddwn fell back with a curse of pain. Before Berrian could
move, Mole sliced the flat of the Sword across Maddwn's
cheek; Maddwn cried out and doubled to the earth. With the
same stroke Mole brought the Sword down on the harness
ring; the blue flash severed the ring toward the center. Bridles
flew. The horses, maddened by the sudden violence near them,
bolted and reared.

"Up!" Mole shouted to Berrian. "Do you want to be tram-
pled?"

Berrian rolled to his feet, face bloodless.

Mole wasted no time with explanation. Out of the corner of
his eye he could see the other outlaws running, daggers drawn.

He slapped Berrian on the shoulder and swung, Sword fly-
ing, onto the back of the nearest horse. He steadied the beast
until Berrian staggered to the side of another horse, then dug
his heels into the horse's flank. The steed reared. Its hooves
chopped air. But soon it sprang forward; with its momentum

Mole slashed the Sword's flat against the backs of the other horses. When he saw that they had scattered, he spurred his horse forward again.

The ground blurred. And the Sword sang as it met two outlaws snatching for Mole's rein. They sank to the ground with groans. Through the wind in his ears, Mole heard Berrian's horse behind and cries from Arien and Fflad ahead. He swerved to miss a third outlaw, shoved the Sword in its sheath, and leaned sideways from the saddle. Almost without slowing the horse, he caught Arien around the waist and heaved her in front of him. Her scream was cut short by Mole's arm around her; she grasped on the saddle ahead of Mole as he pivoted the horse to steady her. Behind them Fflad groped up behind Berrian. Maddwn staggered to his feet. One outlaw chased a horse.

Mole punched his heels to the horse's flank again. The steed's first leap took them over the cooking fire. Its hooves knocked the meat into the flames with a fountain of sparks.

Mole kicked the horse into a gallop. The ground fled beneath them. The hills reared and loomed. Mole guided the horse into a northward ravine; the horse exploded through a thicket, then moved onto open ground. When Berrian's horse caught up with them, Mole's horse sank back to a trot. But Mole applied his boots to the beast's ribs, and the horse ran until the hills closed behind them.

"Mole!" Arien at last caught her breath. "Mole. I thought . . . I thought you had gone mad, that you were really going to leave Berrian with those filthy men. You made me believe your ruse!"

Cringing, Mole replied in a voice he hoped lost itself in the wind, "It wasn't such a hard part to act."

The sky reeled with the turns of ravines.

Berrian's mount jostled with Mole's along the twists of the trail. He leaned forward, expert in his saddle, with Fflad bouncing comically behind. "Forgive my curses!" he shouted. "I thought . . . I thought. . . . Whatever I thought, I'm sorry!"

"Apologies later," Mole yelled back. "Riding now! We've got to put a good distance between Maddwn and us. Or he may make another bargain—a trade for my head, not yours!"

Within an hour the horses tired, and Mole called for a walk. He looked at the hills behind until the horses could be forced back into a trot.

Day drained away with frightening swiftness. Dark came, and the horses stumbled and sidestepped. Their necks were thick with lather. The rocky trail became treacherous, the turns unsure. At last Mole's mount would move no more and halted, as if hobbled, near a hillside copse of gorse.

After unsuccessful attempts to move the horse, Mole climbed from the saddle himself and then helped Arien to the ground.

Her feet crumpled under her. She went to her knees before Mole could support her. "So much riding," she said. "My legs won't be the same again. This wretched stiffness!"

"I've never liked horseback riding," Fflad declared. He sat down suddenly in a patch of grass. "Actually, I wouldn't mind if we got rid of the horses altogether."

Mole considered. "Maybe we should."

"Let them go?" Arien said. "But the outlaws might find them again."

"Certainly," said Mole. "But they won't find them soon, for these horses are too tired to go far even if we let them loose. And if Maddwn's band recovers them, so much the better. They'll have one less reason for following us."

Berrian nodded. "Whatever we decide to do from here, horses won't be practical. If we want to follow Orne, they'll keep us from seeing his tracks. He's gone to the mountains, I think, so horses won't be much use there. And if we decide to return south, horses will only attract notice from goblins and whatever else lives in these wolds."

"We should leave the horses, certainly," Arien agreed, "but we'd better not forget to take the saddlebags with us. I, for one, am starved. What kind of food was in the saddlebags, Mole?"

"I don't know. When I was peering into them, I was in no frame of mind to notice."

Berrian took a saddle pouch from his mount and a large crescent-shaped water skin. From his Mole lifted a pair of leather packs, which seemed heavy enough to be stuffed with rocks.

Arien looked at the sky. "As tired as I am, I don't want to spend the night right here. There must be a place, maybe by that steep bit of hill, where we can be more sheltered."

The others agreed. So they left the horses, Mole with a swift pat to his beast's neck, and made their way along the hill Arien had pointed out. Even in the near darkness Mole could tell that a stream ran against the hill during some season; the hillside was sandy, hollowed, and dotted with spindly trees that reached upward to weave black branches among the stars. Although the place afforded little shelter, it provided comfort with its sandy floor and root-broken wall; they all slumped down beside it with hardly a word.

A wind came up while they passed the water skin around; it moaned in the trees higher on the hill and cast a fine spray of ice and sand down onto them. Yet even with the cold and the bitter leather taste of the water, Mole was content. He found himself reclining into the sand.

Meanwhile Arien investigated the saddlebags. Berrian's, disappointingly, contained nothing more than some rags and a dulled carving knife. But both of Mole's were more interesting: the first brimmed with cheese, dried meat, and hard bread. The second contained what Fflad guessed to be loot from raiding expeditions: some silver coins, a split battle horn with a hawk insignia, and an odd circlet of iron too large to be a bracelet and too small to be a crown. While Arien passed out strips of meat, Fflad took the circlet and weighed it in his hands. He seemed fascinated by the play of starlight on it.

"I think this thing is enchanted," he said as they ate. "I can't say how magical it is or why I think it's magical at all, except that it *feels* that way. Perhaps that nasty lot of outlaws took it from some ancient trove on Fellheath or from a wandering wizard. Whatever this thing is, it's drawn me to it. If nobody objects, I'd like to keep it."

"Have it if you like," Berrian answered. "It doesn't seem magical to me. It's just an iron hoop."

Fflad smiled and slid the circlet into a cloak pocket. "Apparently."

Talk soon turned to other things.

Once he had finished eating, Berrian brushed off his hands, got to his feet, and moved over between Mole and Arien. But he turned to Mole, not Arien. "I have something to say," he began. "About this afternoon. I'm really sorry I called you all those names—"

Mole looked at his fingers. "I might have done the same in your place," he said, grinning. "Or worse."

"Still," Berrian persisted, "I feel terrible about it, especially after you did such a splendid job of saving all our necks—"

"It was marvelous," Fflad broke in. "I couldn't have thought of better myself. And I certainly couldn't have *done* better. When we get back to Thrinedor, I'll write a ballad about it."

Berrian cleared his throat and glared at Fflad. "As I was saying," he resumed, "you did save all of us from those ruffians." His voice went low. "And, blast it all, you especially saved me, even if you scared me to death with that harebrained trick of yours."

Mole dropped a hand on Berrian's shoulder. "I owed you one," he said. "Remember the Thrinefens?"

A brief smile touched Berrian's lips. "I suppose. But still. I've been thinking since we left the river, and more seriously since we left the outlaw camp." He sought Arien's eyes, then Fflad's. "I've come to the conclusion that I've been too rolled up in Berrian, Crown Prince of Thrinedor, and not enough concerned about anybody else. Not that I can stop being a crown prince. But I *can* stop reminding myself that I am."

A pause. The wind seemed to sing across the downs in a beautiful, eerie melody that made Mole's fingers twist around one another. "I think," Mole said, "that it hasn't been all your fault, Berrian. After all, I've acted like a crown prince myself. And I'm not even of royal blood, not that I know of. I don't have an excuse. I've been so worried about trying to catch up with Orne that I've forgotten about the rest of you and about everyone's safety—including yours, Berrian." Another silence followed, during which Fflad and Arien looked at one another, and Fflad nodded slightly.

"I'm willing to turn back to Thrinedor," Mole said.

Berrian looked up. "I'll track Orne for you," he returned.

"Now," Arien cautioned, "don't each of you start arguing the other's part, simply because you've struck an accord. Let's try to be as sensible as possible. Though we've got food now, we're quite lost in these hills. We're off Orne's trail, anyway."

Berrian shifted. Rising to his knees, he pointed northward, to a black triangle under the stars. "True, Arien. But maybe we don't need a trail to follow Orne."

"What do you mean?"

"We're near the northern limits of the Fell Downs, in the very shadow of Mon Cathyn, the Mount of Dragons. If Orne is indeed bound for the land beyond the mountains, and if indeed he has found a guide wise in woodcraft, as seems to be the case, he will take the only pass in the Mon Lluwall that is clear in winter."

"The Dragon Pass," Mole said. "Yes. That makes sense. So we have only to climb the pass to find his trail again."

"But Cathyn Pass?" Fflad said. "I admit it might have some literary interest, considering Sir Rheidol, but still—"

"But the Cathyn dragons are dead." Nonetheless, Mole bit his lip.

"In any case," Berrian said, "today's ride will have closed much of the gap between us and Orne. Perhaps we are even now ahead of him and will be able to stop him in the pass." Berrian looked at Mole. "And as anxious as I am to return to Thrinedor, it would be a shame to turn back now, after we've come this far. We ought to try one more time to catch up with him."

"You're certain you want to?"

Berrian nodded.

"Very well, then," Mole said, clasping Berrian's hand, "we'll start for the Dragon Gate at dawn."

SAGA FOUR

•8•

The White Hawk

NIGHT dropped over the mountain in a sheet. And with the night came frost, soon reinforced by wind, until not even Mole's doeskin cloak could ward off the bite of the high mountain air.

A track they had found in the thickets at the foot of the mountain had been their guide all day, and it had taken them well enough. At twilight they had found themselves far up on the mountain, with a forested ridge behind them and a view of the vastness of the Fell Downs and a glimpse of Fellheath beyond. But still above them granite reaches soared, looking less passible even than they had looked from the downs. That peak seemed to speak to Mole of dragons; Sir Rheidol climbed with him in his thoughts. It was as if time were repeating itself, as if Mole were facing the same task as had the High Prince. Only for Mole a dozen dragons waited.

Yet the scent of pine made Mole think of Mon Ceth, too. Each new view conjured fresh memories: the steep declines thronged with trees and the blast of wind were not unlike Misty Mountain. But in spite of familiar surroundings, Mole could not feel comfortable; the mountain murmured of unseen things, things hovering beyond Mole's ability to sense.

The path had brought them up a ridge to overlook a deep

bowl-shaped valley. Through the valley a fast-flowing stream ran, glistening in the wintery sun. The valley itself was really no more than a gorge between two of Mon Cathyn's lower arms; the path wound up the eastern spur.

At the onset of night, they had halted on a plateau. The valley below vanished into the night, and the southern lands dwindled in dying yellows behind them.

"Sleep?" Arien laughed when Berrian suggested it. "I don't think we'll get much on this hillside in the wind." She glanced at Fflad. "What's more, I can't get the idea of dragons out of my head. I have a sneaking feeling that Sir Rheidol may have missed one or two."

"There were only two dragons," Fflad returned, pulling his cloak around him. "And Prince Rheidol killed both of them. That's what the ballad says, anyway. And since then there hasn't been a dragon in all of the kingdoms. But I do appreciate how Rheidol felt coming up here all alone; it would give me the shivers to think about it if I didn't already have the shivers from the cold. Why couldn't Orne have run away to a warmer place?"

"If you think it's cold now," the Sword said, "wait till morning."

For a time before sleeping, Mole watched the stars. They looked larger here on the mountain than they had from the lowlands. One star in particular, gliding near Orygath and Penegir, flashed like a torch set in the sky. "Serenwawn!" Mole exclaimed aloud, recognizing the star that had seemed to herald disaster for him in the past. "As if things aren't bad enough!" Mole tore his eyes from the sky and gazed instead at the shaggy outlines of the trees until he dropped into an uneasy sleep.

Morning dawned damp, cold, and heavy with fog. The skies were filled with somber clouds. More cloud hid the lands below them; the arm of the mountain seemed to be a headland jutting into a cold sea. Shreds of fog waxed the branches of the evergreens and drifted along the forest floor like grey birds. Yet though a dreadful cold set in, the wind died with the coming of the light.

"What I would give for a hot breakfast!" Arien exclaimed. Her teeth rattled as she passed out cheese. Mole offered to trade cloaks with her, but she refused.

"Bother winter!" Berrian said when he had eaten.

"And bother this miserable fog while you're at it," Fflad added. "I'd looked forward to seeing that valley and to gazing back on Fellheath. We couldn't see much last night; I thought this morning would be different. We're high enough to see Thrinedor from here."

"View or not, we must move on," Mole said. "This is a perfect day to overtake Orne or wait for him at the pass. Berrian, have you seen any tracks?"

"A few. But the ground's too frozen to tell whether they're Orne's."

Mole started out in the lead, planting the ash staff in the cold sod of the trail. Berrian walked at his heels, and whenever Mole slowed down, Berrian moved ahead. The reverse would happen a moment later as Mole pushed ahead. Arien suggested that one or the other ought to lead, but neither listened; the jostling for the lead was continual, and it kept them moving at a good pace. The country fled by.

The mist below seemed to thicken rather than lift as the day went on, and overhead Mon Cathyn's peak was barely visible through cloud. They saw no bird or animal the whole morning, although Berrian found deer tracks in the mud beside the trail.

The path steepened and moved up a pine-covered wall in switchbacks. Eventually it became so narrow and the grade so steep, that Mole allowed Berrian, as the better tracker, to lead. He knew they approached the peak because the pines had thinned and were very small, and those there were were bent almost double by the wind. Rock slides appeared to their right and left; one covered their path, forcing them to pick their way across unsteady stones. When Berrian stumbled, one of the outlaws' packs was carried away down the hill by loose rocks.

The trees vanished altogether. Snowfields appeared. Ragged slopes lifted to the sky. Mole's head began to swim, and each time they crossed an icy patch on the trail, his legs began to ache. He was glad to round a lip of stone and come onto a tableland blanketed with snow. The trail went across the flat toward the summit, weaving among the largest boulders and the highest mounds of snow until it vanished into the misty distance. They halted there on the edge of the tableland before going on. The view was breathtaking.

Falling away like the immense folds of a giant's cloak were gorges and ridges, vales and hidden coombs, all veiled in mist and patched with forest. No glimpse of the Fell Downs or of Fellheath was possible because they were covered by a quilt of cloud. But for a moment the sun flashed through the upper fogs, and a dozen golden stars appeared on the mountainside, lakes in the deeps of the mountain woods.

"This view is worth the climb," Arien said. "But I would have preferred seeing it out a window from a chair by the fire."

"Yes," Fflad said. "But few cottages are built in such wilds. Can you sense the greatness of this mountain? It's like a poem! And this peak isn't the only one, either; to both east and west there are more peaks connected with this one, like a great wall. Like a wall, all smoking with mist. It would make a lovely poem. A wall of secret mist-mountains—"

"Your imagery isn't far off, my boy," said the Sword. "The Mon Lluwall do form a wall, in a loose sense, and Mon Cathyn is the gate."

Soon they started over the flat. Mole had seen few places more bleak than that plateau. The path led toward the peak; it swerved to the left to face a wall of ice-broken cliffs that formed the westward face of the mountain. In the wall a cleft, which might be a narrow pass or canyon, opened up before them.

Pinnacles of sheer rock broke upward all around; even the peak sank behind the ice-decked rock. A stone's throw from the opening, Mole could see that the path wound into the dark depths of the gorge. He hoped to escape the wind between the walls of rock, but instead, when they stepped in, they found that the air grew colder and the wind wilder, as if this stone itself bred iciness and generated wind.

"I hear something," Arien said, just inside the opening. "Something like howling or moaning."

"Nonsense!" Mole told her. He stared into the narrow darkness. "You're probably hearing the wind in the rocks."

All the same, he did hear cries that sounded like wolves in the distance.

Fflad placed a hand on the rock. "This canyon doesn't seem exactly natural, does it? Maybe the part of the poem that said the mountain split wasn't exaggerating. Look at the rocks. See how they've been pulled apart, as if by an earthquake?"

"They ought to have been pulled apart a bit more," Arien said. "The place is only two paces wide if it's an inch." Her eyes flicked to Mole's. "It'll be a narrow squeeze. Is there another way?"

"Not unless you want to climb Cathyn Peak, where the dragons used to live. No. This is the only way. Besides, it's the way Orne will come, or did come."

Berrian frowned. "Let's not frighten ourselves by waiting," he said. "Let's go on."

In the cleft only a greyish strip of sky appeared above their heads. The light grew dimmer after the first turn of the cliffs, and Mole could barely make out Berrian in front of him. The way seemed to pinch in on them; there were places where Mole had to squeeze sideways between outcroppings of rock. Debris littered the floor—pebbles, broken icicles, and smears of snow. At one point Mole thought he saw a feather on the ice, but because of the dimness he could not be certain.

Imagining they were being followed, Mole kept looking behind him. But he saw nothing, heard nothing—though he noted a few dark birds winging overhead. It was curious, he thought, that there should be such large birds here on the mountain peak. The birds seemed too large to be hawks or eagles.

It began to snow. The snow dusted Mole's head and shoulders in a fine white powder. The moaning in the rocks grew louder.

"We ought to come out soon," Arien said. Her voice resounded from the walls. "It seems as if we've walked a thousand miles in this place."

As she spoke, they rounded a crook in the way. A blaze of white light and a wall of wind met them. Mole saw Berrian ahead silhouetted against the brightness. The cliffs fell back, and big, thick flakes of snow struck Mole's face. When he brought an arm up to shelter his eyes, he saw that they had emerged onto a narrow ledge overlooking the far slopes of the mountain, which were thick with snow. Far to the north were valleys where snow clouds hovered and snowflakes danced. Lightnings flickered in the distant haze. An ancient excitement hovered in the air and trembled in the mountain.

Mole realized he looked at the land of the inner mountains, a land so distant from his accustomed world that he had heard little of it even in legends. As the others gathered around him, he gazed out over the endless ranges of the northern mountains and wondered, for the first time, whether the Emperor that Orne sought did indeed live beyond that snow-covered infinity.

But Mole's eyes caught something else, something nearer.

Against the backdrop of snow, the man was almost invisible, for he was clad entirely in white. Standing as if molded of snow, he faced toward the inner mountains. Snow caked the lower hem of his cloak, and strapped across his back was a slender bow the color of ice and a quiver of frost-tipped arrows. Only threads of tawny hair alerted Mole to his presence.

Mole slipped the Sword from its sheath. He nudged Berrian and motioned to Fflad. Berrian's hand went to his breast, and Fflad drew his dagger and moved in behind Mole's shoulder.

"Hullo!" Mole said above the wind.

The stranger started and pivoted. Before Mole could raise the Sword, the man dropped to his knee and snapped an arrow to his bow.

Mole stared. "We mean you no harm if you mean none—"

Pale fingers tightened around the bow. "If you mean no harm, sheath your weapons," a voice called back.

Mole slowly sheathed the Sword.

When Berrian and Fflad had done likewise, the stranger removed his arrow and lowered his bow. The stranger's face, Mole saw, was boyish and round. He decided that he had misjudged the stranger; rather than a man, this was a boy, a boy no older than Fflad by the size of him.

Blue eyes flamed. "Who are you?"

"We are travelers," Berrian answered, "from Thrinedor."

The boy's grip on the bow relaxed, but only a little. Mole

noticed a pad of cloth, like a thick bandage, around the boy's left forearm.

"And you?" Berrian prodded.

"I'm a traveler, too. From Vivrandon."

"And your name?"

The boy's red lips tightened. "You've not given me yours."

Mole started to answer, but Berrian broke in. "I am Berrian, son of Ellarwy of Thrinedor," he stated. "And these are my companions. Now, who might you be, boy?"

The stranger's cheeks reddened, and he frowned. "To begin with, I'm not a boy. My name in Merani Felleira, and I'm a princess. At least I used to be."

"Oh," said Mole. "I see. Pardon our mistake; the snow is fierce, and it's hard to see. You're of noble blood from Vivrandon? You wouldn't be related to Prince Ichodred—"

"I wouldn't be," Merani replied, "if my mother hadn't married his uncle." Her eyes darkened. "He's my cousin."

"I take it you claim no family tie," Fflad put in.

Merani lifted her bow. "I'm Ichodred's enemy and will be until one of us dies. If you are friends of his or of his Black Counselor, beware! I have a swift bow!"

"Ichodred is our enemy, too, though I'm sure our enmity isn't as fierce as yours. Now tell me, Merani Felleira, why are you here?"

"What business is that of yours?" Merani asked. "I mean, I might be here as well as anywhere else. And," she added, thrusting out her chin, "I might ask you the same question. After all, no one comes to the Dragon Gate without reason."

"Our reason," Mole sighed, "has long gone or is as yet to pass the Dragon Gate. We seek a friend of ours, a boy named Orne."

Merani's hand flew to her throat. She dropped her bow and rose to her feet. "Orne!" she exclaimed. "Orne?"

Mole nodded. Merani's eyes touched his, then moved to the others in turn. "Then you must be Mole," she said, in a very different voice. "And you must be Arien; Orne said you had lovely hair. And you're Fflad. Ah, yes. You've got to be Fflad —that twist in your lips is unmistakable." Merani wrinkled her nose at Berrian. "I wouldn't know your name if you hadn't told me. I don't think Orne ever mentioned you."

"Orne? You know Orne?"

"You're the person who helped him across Fellheath so we couldn't catch up with him!" Fflad said.

"Where is Orne now?" Arien asked.

Merani looked down at her bow, which the snow had begun to cover. She plucked it up, pinched the moisture from the string, and put it back in her pack. All the while her eyes were on the north. The increasing curtain of snowflakes hid most of the mountains. "He went north," she answered simply. "I told him I couldn't go any farther away from Vivrandon than this, with Ichodred still in power. I told him I couldn't go with him anymore. But he has a mind of his own. He went on."

"To the north?"

"How could you let him go?" Arien demanded.

Merani glared at Arien. "How could I stop him?"

Mole moved to the edge of the ledge. He saw footprints in the drifts, now fading with new flakes, winding down through the rocks. "Merani," he said sternly, "how long ago did he leave?"

"Not long. An hour, perhaps."

"Then we must follow him."

"Follow him?" Merani went to Mole and looked up at him. "Why follow him? You'd have a hard time overtaking him. He has drive, you know; he has almost run all the way from Fellheath. And even if you caught him, I doubt if you'd be able to change his mind about trying to find the Emperor. I couldn't."

"But he'll listen to us. When he knows we've followed him all this way, he'll realize he should turn back."

"He already knows you've followed him," she said. "When I met him on Fellheath, one of the first things he told me was that his friends would be searching for him. Since that time I've sent Cwyller to spy on you. You've been on our heels since the southern parts of Fellheath. But Cwyller didn't see you in the Fell Downs. I don't know why."

Arien pushed in between Mole and Merani. "You knew Orne was running away all the time, running away into *this*," Arien tossed a hand toward the north, "and still you helped him keep out of our reach. How could you do that? Why did you?''

Merani turned a shoulder to Arien. "Orne had his quest, as I have mine," she said. "Who am I to hold him back? How could I? And can you blame me for helping him, for seeing him safely this far? I could have done nothing but what I did!''

"You can help us now.''

"Help you do what?" Merani's head snapped toward Mole. "Help you track Orne down like an animal and drag him in ropes back to Thrinedor? Help you thwart Orne's wish to go north, when I've listened to him explain his need over and over? No. No, I can't do that, no matter what you do to me, because I won't.''

Silence followed.

Mole grimaced. "Perhaps you're right, Merani Felleira. But still,'' Mole curled his fingers around the ash staff, "but still, the thought of Orne perishing in that wilderness, noble reasons or not—''

"How do you know he won't find what he seeks?" Merani answered. "*He* seems confident enough that he'll reach the place his mind paints for him. And he has just enough stubbornness to make it over the mountains. All of us know that.'' Merani's voice faltered a little when she went on. "And if you think about it, Orne will join Llan and find the Emperor one way or the other.''

The snow beat against Mole's cheeks, against his eyelids, against the hair covering his ears. The flakes collected in the hollows between his knuckles as, squeezing the staff in both hands, he brought it back to rest against his chest. He could feel vaguely that the others were looking at him, but he ignored them. Instead he fixed his eyes on an imaginary shape, the size of a snowflake, that faded into the shadow of wind-drifted mountains.

"Would I be presuming on our new friendship," Berrian ventured, touching Mole's shoulder, "to suggest we start back for Thrinedor?''

Mole stiffened, then shook his head. "No. No, you wouldn't.''

Berrian grinned. "I'm glad, Mole."

Mole turned to Merani. "In spite of what I said before, you did Orne a great service in bringing him across Vivrandon safely. For your help we thank you. And we would be happy to have you travel south with us as far as you wish to go."

Merani nodded. "I'll go with you as far as Fellhaven, at least. But I must go to Fellhaven. I promised Lord Daerwyn that I would go there at least once a month. Otherwise he worries about me, though I don't see why." Merani pressed her lips and scanned the snow-veiled sky. "I'll be ready to leave just as soon as Cwyller comes back. I sent him to follow Orne for a few miles. He should be coming soon—"

"Who's Cwyller?" Berrian asked, squinting into the snow. "Another former noble?"

Merani had no chance to answer.

Something whispered across Mole's cheek. Mole pitched forward. He clamped his hand to the stinging stripe on his face. Through the blur of his eyes, he saw Merani kneel to loose an arrow. He heard a thud, a groan, then a thump of something heavy striking the snow. Pulling his hand away, he saw snow-peppered blood and glimpsed vaguely, between his fingers, an arrow shaft protruding from the ground near him.

Arien ran to him, but he pushed her away. Berrian's sword screamed from its sheath. Mole heard shouts. Whirling around, toward the pass, he saw a frost-feathered arrow in a body garbed in bearskin.

Then he knew what was happening.

"Outlaws!" he shouted in dismay. "Outlaws! Merani, Arien, get back! Berrian, watch yourself! They're coming out of the pass!"

Despite Mole's warning, Merani fitted another arrow to her bow. Arien, too, did not retreat to the relative safety of the higher rocks; she moved instead to the body of the fallen outlaw and rose wielding a long black knife. Mole shouted at her to keep back, but he had time only to draw the Sword before the first outlaw was on him.

Mole parried the outlaw's blow, then struck downward toward the man's knees. The outlaw barred the stroke. He returned another. Mole heard Berrian shout something. Out of the corner of his eye, he saw that one outlaw, Maddwn, had driven Berrian back against the rocks. Mole ducked his opponent's next blow, dived past him, and arrived at Berrian's side. He shoved his blade between Maddwn's sword and Berrian's head.

Maddwn's eyes flashed. He snarled and turned toward Mole. But Mole, seeing trouble elsewhere, darted away with Maddwn at his heels. Merani's arrows had not stopped an outlaw's advance. Instead the ruffian struggled with her; he plucked the bow from her hands and snapped it in two. But before he could drop the fragments, Mole's Sword met his shoulder. He staggered away and stumbled over the fallen outlaw archer.

"Back to the rocks!" Mole yelled to Merani. "Get back!" This time Merani obeyed. With a swift glance at her broken bow, she plucked Arien's wrist and drew her back. Mole watched until they reached the end of the ledge.

"The outlaw!" the Sword shrilled. "Behind you!"

Mole leaped aside. He spun around in air and found himself face-to-face with Maddwn, whose sword moved toward him. It glanced off Mole's hip. "Scoundrel!" Maddwn raged, deep eyes blazing. "Robber! You will pay for what you did, Moleander of Thrinedor!"

Grimly Mole parried. The Sword shuddered. Mole's arm buckled at the force of Maddwn's blow. The notion flickered in Mole's mind that it would be useless to battle Maddwn directly, for his rage fed his strength, and Mole could never hope to overpower him. So before Maddwn could strike again, Mole sprang away.

Beside Maddwn, two warriors remained. One fought Berrian near the rock gate; Berrian, though staggering, seemed to be getting the better of his foe. Fflad, however, was fighting an uncommonly large outlaw who had cornered him on the edge of the cliff. Fflad's dagger clinked against the knife of his opponent. But at every stroke Fflad sank nearer to his knees, clutching his side with his elbow.

Mole had no time to challenge the outlaw; Maddwn followed only steps behind him. So, breaking into a run, Mole bellowed for Fflad to duck. The moment Fflad dropped to the

ground, Mole jumped and landed with both feet on the
outlaw's back. The kick sent the ruffian somersaulting over
the snowy brink; Mole shuddered when he heard the splinter-
ing of timber.

Fflad scrambled quickly aside. But Mole, breathless from
his fall, could not get to his feet. It was all he could do to
wriggle to his hands and knees and throw up the Sword to
block the blow he knew was coming. Because his resistance
was feeble, Maddwn almost knocked the Sword from his grip,
and the backstroke met Mole full in the chest. It drove the
breath from his body and sent him spinning to his back.
Quickly he rolled over in the snow, heard Maddwn's sword
slash behind him, bolted to his feet, and assumed a wheezing
stance.

He used the last tight reach of his breath to call to Fflad.
"Back to the rocks! Back to Merani and Arien!" Fflad,
watching helplessly, nodded and backed away, limping.

Maddwn charged, and Mole slid away toward the cliffs,
toward where Berrian's foe had crumpled to the earth. Berrian
threw out a bloodstained sword to guard Mole's retreat. But
before Mole reached him, his features drained, his shoulders
drew together, and he dropped into the snow.

"Now, rogue, it's you and me!" Maddwn snarled. He
plunged toward Mole. "Move aside! Or will you protect that
foolish prince of yours even when he's dead!"

"He isn't dead," Mole sputtered, bringing up the Sword.
"And dead or alive, I won't abandon him to you. If you want
him, kill me first!"

"Nothing," Maddwn sneered, raising his sword, "would
give me more pleasure."

The weapon crashed across Mole's left shoulder. Mole par-
ried, struck upward, but Maddwn towered beyond his reach.
Maddwn's blade swung upward and hovered, waiting, and
Mole knew that the fall of the sword would bring his end.

When the scream came, Mole thought it was his own. But
with it came other sounds, sounds Mole perceived only
vaguely above the pounding of blood in his ears. He looked up
to see Maddwn's sword wilting backwards in the face of a
winged fury the color of snow that screeched, hovered, struck.

But Mole did not waste his chance in surprise. He exploded forward and drove his Sword into the now-exposed bearskin tunic.

Maddwn's curse died in his throat as he doubled lifeless into the snow.

It was only after Mole dropped the Sword that he realized his life had been saved by Merani's hawk.

· 9 ·

The Loremaster Prince

Two weeks passed before they reached the downs again.

The first week they spent in the high timber on the Vivrandon side of the Dragon Pass. There, in a cavity among roots, away from the wind, Merani supervised the construction of a lean-to of logs and pine branches, in front of which she built a small fire. The snow stopped falling on the second day, so the place was not really cold. Yet Mole didn't like the look of the swath of white he glimpsed beyond the limbs. He was anxious to be off, for his own wounds from the battle with the outlaws —the scratch on his cheek, the bruises on his chest—healed quickly with rest, food, and fire.

Fflad and Berrian, however, hadn't fared as well as Mole. Fflad had a slit in his tunic and a long cut along his ribs to match it. When Merani and Arien bandaged him, he winced with pain, though he tried to be cheerful. Berrian was worse off still; he had scarcely been awake during the return through the pass, and he collapsed before they reached the forest. Two deep wounds, one in his leg and one in his shoulder, had cost him much blood. His skin was sallow, and his eyes, on the few occasions he opened them, hazy. His cheeks wasted to hollowness until even Arien admitted he was no longer handsome. A fever seized him on the second day, and until it broke on the fourth, he writhed in his bandages and alternately wept to his father for having gone away and muttered that he wanted to see Mole. Though it did little to ease his impatience, Mole kept at Berrian's side.

For Mole the most pleasant part of their stay in the trees was Merani's hawk, Cwyller. He would have taken an immediate liking to the bird, he decided, even if it hadn't saved his life. Cwyller was large for a hawk, almost the size of an eagle, and perfectly white. He was not as noisy as the falcons Mole had known, but he was just as restless; his bright cold eyes moved ceaselessly. He would rest on Merani's arms for only a few minutes before heaving away from her, perching on a tree, and disappearing beyond the trees for whole afternoons. After observing the hawk's movements for several days, Mole came to the conclusion that the bird was as intelligent as a person. He asked Merani whether Cwyller ever spoke with her, but she ignored his question.

As soon as she repaired her bow, Merani left them. Outlaws, she told Mole, rarely all moved together. She was certain Maddwn had friends down the trail. And she meant to find out how many of them there were and where they waited. Mole insisted he go in her place, but she refused. He said he would go with her, then. But she slipped away from them one dawn without waking anyone up. Mole wanted to follow her, but Arien quietly asked him to stay and help with Berrian. And Mole could not refuse.

After the third day Berrian began to improve. His fever drained away on the fourth, he could sit up on the fifth, and he took jaunts through the wood with Mole on the sixth. Yet although he said he was ready to start for Thrinedor on the seventh day, his complexion remained wan, and when Mole clasped his hand, his knuckles felt brittle, twiglike almost, and his grip was soft.

On the eve of the eighth day Merani returned as silently as she had left. She reported that together she and Cwyller had observed no less than fifty outlaws encamped on the edge of the mountain and along the trail down. Mole suggested trying to slip by them, but Fflad pointed out that there were really too many of them for secrecy. Merani told them, further, that

she had heard of another way down the mountain, a longer
trail that wound along the face of the Mon Lluwal and arrived
at the Fell Downs far to the northwest, almost to the River
Woldwash, the west boundary of Vivrandon. No outlaws
would be on guard there. The greatest drawback of the plan,
Merani admitted, was that the trail would take them far out of
their way. But there was little choice.

They left the pine wood the next morning.

The second week they spent on the trail, an almost invisible
track that rounded the shoulders of Mon Cathyn, dipped
across a forested gorge, then climbed along the timberline of
the mountains to the west. Going was slow, for the way was
narrow and steep, and Berrian, despite a valiant effort, could
not travel far without resting. Snow fell off and on. Their
food ran low, and only rabbits from Merani's bow and
pigeons from her hawk kept them from starving. Mole felt
almost as restless as he had been when they remained in camp.
Somehow uneasiness, like the promise of a storm, buzzed in
the air. Their progress, measured only by the curves of the
mountain, seemed slow.

In addition, Mole found himself obsessed with thoughts
of Vivrandon, the Black Counselor, and Prince Ichodred.
Shivering at night, he dreamed of sorcerers and unnamed
beings astride fire-eyed horses. And even when his thoughts
turned to other things, he found himself fingering the Sword.

He tried asking Merani about Vivrandon; after all, she had
been born there. But she only shrugged at his inquiries or
ignored them altogether, until Mole determined to keep his
thoughts to himself. The only comment Merani made about
Rathvidrian was on the day the trail twisted down toward the
flatlands. Cwyller had just returned from a flight over the Fell
Downs.

"Rathvidrian is almost directly south of us now," she said
when Cwyller, perched on her shoulder, finished his customary chattering. "I think Cwyller has seen trouble there and
along the river both east and west of the fortress."

"Trouble?" Mole squinted southward. "What kind of
trouble?"

Without answering, Merani started down the trail.

"Any kind of trouble you like," the Sword said. "War,

famine, outlaws, goblins, burnings. It all happens in Vivrandon.''

"If it's war," Berrian said with a pale frown, "Ichodred has made some move against us. Or," he added darkly, "some king has disobeyed the High King and has moved against Ichodred himself.''

"Any way you look at it," Mole said, "it won't be good for us.''

Late afternoon brought them from the last forested ridge into the Downs. After Mole scanned the area for outlaws and hawk riders, they bedded down in willows near a frozen creek.

Merani woke the next morning more cheerful than she had yet been. Her ruddy face lit with pleasure as she sniffed the dawn wind, and the frost in her eyes melted a little as she watched the sun wash grey across the downs. "I can smell the Fellflood," she said in a quiet voice. "We're not more than two days away from it. That means," her voice sank, "we're only three days from home.''

Since Cwyller hinted Rathvidrian lay in the south, they started off in a westerly direction, along a stream-threaded valley that Merani said would bring them to the River Woldwash. After a lengthy discussion the night before, they had determined to follow a plan suggested by Berrian, to avoid as much of Vivrandon as possible by cutting west across to the Woldwash and over it into Sharicom, where, when they reached Ranath Sharicom, Berrian could ask for horses from King Cashma to take them across Northmarch back to Thrinedor. Merani, of course, would accompany them only as far as the river, for she would not leave Vivrandon.

Merani seemed cheerful. She soon forgot about keeping the lead, and Mole and Berrian moved ahead of her. She dropped back to join Arien, who soon set her to talking. Matching strides ahead, Mole and Berrian quit their own conversation to listen.

"I've always thought it would be wonderful to be a princess," Arien said. "Didn't you say that you were a princess?''

"I *used* to be—sort of," Merani replied. "At least I have royal blood. My father was Fifraneira, son of Fifran II, King of Vivrandon. My father was the younger brother of Ichodron, the last king at Ranath Vivrandon before Ichodred.

My mother was royal, too. I know that even though she never
talked about where she came from, except to say she was born
in a secret village in the Mon Dau. She was beautiful, fair-
skinned wtih hair the color of flax. She had to be a princess.
Or an enchantress.''

"An enchantress?'' Glancing back, Mole saw that Arien
had taken the small white book from her cloak and was
holding it against her. She looked up at Mole but asked
Merani, "Did you live at Ranath Vivrandon, then?''

"We never lived there, even before it became Rathvidrian.
We had a great stone house on the moors—it's destroyed now,
thanks to Ichodred.'' Merani's eyes grew cold. "May he
burn!''

"Your house,'' Arien said quickly, "what was it like?''

"It was beautiful, the most beautiful building in all Vivrandon. Trees grew on a creek nearby—they were full of pigeons
and doves. After my mother died, my father took me hawking
there—our hawks were of a special breed, they were white-
feathered and much more intelligent than the birds the other
hawk lords kept. We never starved them in order to later
reward them for cruelty, as the other lords did. My father and
I hunted as well as hawked; my father had grown up in the
eastern wilds, near Fellhaven, so he was almost a woodmaster.
He taught me to track, to forage, and to shoot the bow. Now,
Arien, am I boring you?''

"Not at all, Merani. Please go on.''

"My father was an enemy of Prince Ichodred in court.'' At
this point Mole began to listen more carefully. "He saw
Ichodred's black plans for Vivrandon and warned Ichodred's
father, Ichodron, not to let Ichodred have the crown. He
wanted Ichodron to renounce Ichodred as crown prince.
Ichodron never did, but my father's objections infuriated
Ichodred. So it wasn't surprising that as soon as the king died,
Prince Ichodred assumed the throne and sent warriors to capture my father.''

"Fortunately,'' Merani went on, with hardly a breath, "my
father spotted Ichodred's hawks and surmised that Ichodred
had made himself king. We escaped on horseback into the
moors. That was in the autumn a year ago. We tried first to
reach Fellhaven. But one horse went lame. Then, Ichodred's

army marched up Fellflood Vale, burning estates of those hawk lords who had, like my father, opposed him. We feared Fellhaven would be captured before we could reach it. So we started across Fellheath toward Thrinedor. But the first storm of winter struck, and we had little food; the snow deepened, and our other horse died." Merani's face darkened. "My father caught a fever. He couldn't walk. We had no horses, no shelter, nothing with which to build a fire. I did what I could, but . . ."

Arien touched Merani's arm. "I'm sorry."

Merani only frowned. "I vowed, while I watched my father die, that I would revenge him." Her fists tightened until they were white. "I swore never to leave Vivrandon until Ichodred and his Black Counselor had been overthrown and slain. So far I've kept my pledge. And I don't plan to break it."

Mole could not imagine that Merani would.

"How have you lived since then?" Arien asked.

"Daerwyn of Fellhaven gives me supplies. He wanted me to stay at Fellhaven when I first came there. But I refused; I prefer to wander the moors. Cwyller, my father's swiftest hawk, found me the first time I went to Fellhaven. Since that time he and I have been together. We've had our own war against Ichodred. I shot two of his riders last summer. I'd kill more, but most of them are deathless—"

"Then it's true," Mole interrupted, suddenly feeling hollow. "Deathless?"

"Some of them are. I would be protected myself if I weren't a girl. You act as if it's something new. But it isn't. Those of the royal house of Vivrandon have been protected for as long as I can remember. I don't know why. Or how. But it's enchantment, I've heard, a spell cast in Ichodron's time. My father himself could not be harmed by a sword." Merani's lips curled downward. "But he died with a fever."

Fflad interrupted Mole's reply. He pushed his way between Merani and Arien and snatched Mole's sleeve, his cheeks ashen. "I don't want to alarm any of you," he said in a low voice, "but we're being followed—don't look back. I would have said something before, but all of you were talking so fast, and I didn't want to interrupt."

"We're being followed?" Berrian hissed. "By whom?"

"I don't know. But he's getting closer."

"He? There's only one?" Mole halted so abruptly, Fflad nearly collided with him. "If there's only one, I dare say the five of us are a match for him—if he's an enemy at all. Berrian, get ready with your sword, but don't draw unless he does. Fflad, keep back." He glanced at Arien and Merani. "You two girls stay back, too. Use your bow if you want, Merani, but remember, you're not protected by the enchantment of Vivrandon."

Mole saw that the man Fflad had described was scarcely a stone's throw behind them. He seemed unafraid of them; his strides soon bridged the distance between them. Mole could not fear a lone man, but he was wary of the man's apparent confidence. He steadied Berrian with a glance and held his ground, his hand ready at his hip.

The man wore what was obviously a uniform, but its color was no uniform of Vivrandon. His cloak was a dark shade of brown, almost black. It fell only partway below his waist. His yellow tunic, loose-fitting and unbelted, was stitched with brown griffins and dragons. Above his snow-speckled boots hung a naked scimitar and a narrow iron battle horn, both of which curved at their tips. The man's coloring reminded Mole, oddly, of Gareth; the man's eyes gleamed like polished ebony from beneath black brows and an earth-brown forehead.

"Sharicom," Berrian whispered as the man halted. "Sharicom."

"You are travelers," the man assumed, nodding toward Mole.

"Yes. And you," Mole returned, "are you any friend of Ichodred's?"

The man's eyes moved from Mole to Berrian and from Berrian to Fflad. "No more than you are, by the look of you. I am Ashrad, scout for His Highness Cashma, King of Sharicom."

Mole laughed and stepped forward. "Cashma? Then you are a friend." He took the dark hand and shook it. "For we are adventurers from Thrinedor on our way to your king's stronghold—"

"You won't find him there," Ashrad said. His teeth disappeared into a frown. "And if you continue to follow this

valley, you'll come upon the troop of Vivrandon horsemen
that hounded us across Woldwash. I came to warn you of
that—I saw that you were not of Vivrandon."

"We appreciate your trouble, sir," Berrian said. "I am Berrian, Crown Prince of Thrinedor. I would like to speak to
your king."

"Crown Prince of Thrinedor," the scout echoed. "Sire,
word came from Thrinedor that you were lost, presumed kidnapped or dead."

Berrian stiffened. His lip twitched, and his hand went to his
shoulder as if his wound had begun to hurt again. "I'm not
dead. And I have not been kidnapped—at least not in the ordinary fashion." Berrian looked sidelong at Mole. "I must
return to Thrinedor at once. Where is King Cashma?"

"South of here. Just a few miles."

Mole's eyes widened. "He's here? In Vivrandon?" There
was only one conclusion he could draw. "Your king has
crossed the Woldwash with an army," he said dully, "to attack Rathvidrian."

"But he can't do that!" Berrian burst out.

"But he has."

"This is serious business," Berrian said, "very serious
business. Your king was under a ban from the High King not
to cross the Woldwash, not to attack Vivrandon until spring.
If he has disobeyed that command, his crown could be
forfeit."

"Kings of Sharicom have defied the High Throne before,"
Ashrad said, in a tone that was decidedly cooler. "And he has
his reasons, not the least of which are the dozens of herders in
our worlds killed by Ichodred's riders."

Mole and Berrian looked at one another, then Mole shook
his head. "I almost wish," he said, "that you'd not told us of
war. It is grave news."

"No. It's not bad news. It's good news." Merani, her bow
collected loosely in her hand, moved ahead of the others. She
addressed the scout. "I say it's about time that somebody
challenged Ichodred. Even if your king defied higher authority
to do it, I admire him for it. If somebody's fighting Ichodred,
I want to be there. Take me back to your camp. I'll offer
myself as an archer."

The scout smiled. "We need no maiden warriors, my lady."

Merani lifted her chin. "I am Merani Felleira. And by the white hawk, I've slain more hawk riders than you."

The scout's eyebrows fell. "Then you may return with me to my king and offer your service to him."

"I, too, offer service." Mole steadied himself with the staff. "Your king will need all the help he can get."

"Mole," Arien burst out, "don't go. You can't go." She came to him and placed a hand on his arm. "Please. It's too dangerous. By himself against Vivrandon, Cashma has no chance to win!"

"His chances, at least," Mole said, tearing his eyes from Arien, "will be a little better if I go. The Sword that slew Ammar must come to bear against the Black Counselor."

"I, too, shall come," Berrian said. "I've fought in no battles, but if I am to become King of Thrinedor, I must learn how." He clamped a hand on Mole's shoulder and added, "And Mole shall not go alone."

"Indeed he won't," Fflad said, dropping a hand to Mole's other shoulder. "I'll come, too, though I'm better at poetry than fighting. I'll come," he added to Ashrad, "if your king can spare a sword for me to fight with."

Mole turned to Fflad. "You've made a valiant offer, Fflad, but I think you ought to stay out of the battle to protect Arien."

"To protect Arien?" Arien returned. "What if Arien doesn't need any protecting? If Merani can be an archer, so can I. I'm fair with a bow. And I'm not as fragile as you seem to think."

"But you are a lady, Arien," Berrian protested. "Ladies aren't warriors."

"None of you objected when Merani volunteered," Arien countered. "Is there a difference between us?"

Berrian folded his arms. Mole wanted to reply, but he felt Merani's frosty gaze on him.

"Yes, I'll come with you," Arien said in a quieter voice. She pushed her hair back over her shoulder, and Mole noticed that she carried the little white book in her hand. "I will come," she repeated with effort, as if fighting some inner battle. "I will come with you, Mole." Her eyes lifted to Mole's. "After all, I've been in battles before."

They set off at once. The scout led them southward, upward across a range of ripplelike hills topped with brush. He told them that the place King Cashma would strike camp was not far, that they would reach the valley before nightfall, if they encountered no hawk riders on the way.

They said nothing for the first part of the journey. Yet their walk was by no means silent; the crunch of their footfalls across snowfields was punctuated by the click of weapons and gear. Mole's doeskin cloak hissed across the shoots of dead grass and rattled against the twigs of an occasional patch of bracken. As he walked, Mole fancied that he could see birds floating in the high reaches.

At midafternoon Cwyller returned, dropping out of the clouds like an enormous snowflake. He landed on Merani's shoulder and began to chirp to her. Merani's face went taut with understanding, but she did not pass on what she had learned from her hawk.

"I can't believe Cashma would disobey the High King," Mole said eventually. "Didn't his underlords tell him of the council's decision? Didn't Gwarthan tell him that many of the Vivrandon warriors are deathless in battle?"

Scanning the clouds, Ashrad nodded. "He knows."

"Then how can he even think of attacking Rathvidrian?"

The scout paused. "Have you heard the prophecy?"

"We've heard it," Berrian snapped. "Both Mole and I were at the council when Gwarthan spoke it. As I remember, it made little sense. It talked of princes becoming knaves and knaves princes. There was also something about the dead becoming alive again."

"Indeed. But what is nonsense to you is sacred to King Cashma. For part of the prophecy has come true. A knave has become a prince." Ashrad noted both Mole and Berrian's expressions of surprise. "Shortly after the wizard Gwarthan arrived from Thrinedor, the king found a son who was lost as an infant and thought dead these many years. A boy became a prince overnight."

"That seems a shaky fulfillment to me," Mole returned.

"After all, the boy never really stopped being a prince."

The scout, hurrying onward, chose not to reply.

"I guess that makes what I thought silly," Fflad said. "And it's a pity. I thought myself rather clever for having come up with my own interpretation of the prophecy's fulfillment." Fflad shrugged and sighed. "It was a nice thought."

"What was your idea?" Mole asked.

Fflad looked up. "You know that part about the prince becoming a knave and the knave a prince? I thought that it sort of came true—I know this sounds silly—when you and Prince Berrian became friends. . . ."

Berrian and Mole looked at each other but said nothing.

Evening drew on. A fog rose with the setting of the sun. In the silent hour of walking before they reached the camp, it was all Mole could do to keep his eyes from wandering too deep into the darkness. The flesh on his arms crawled.

He thought he heard the keening of hawks in the wind.

From the last hilltop the watchfires were visible only as gold blotches in the fabric of night. It seemed as if everything in the valley below was under water because of the mist. Mole could only determine the size of the Sharicom army by the number of fires; he counted twenty up and down the valley, but some may have been hidden by hills or by the thickness of the starless night. When they reached the valley floor, firelit shapes rose up to challenge them, but Ashrad shouted his name and waved them back; they receded like ghosts into the fuzzy light around their fires.

Once inside the camp, the companions grouped more tightly together. Mole could see little more than the spark of scattered fires, but he could hear the wicker of horses, the creak of grounded spears moved by the wind, the hiss of flames rising through cooking grates. The atmosphere, in addition, was tainted with the scent of horses and iron and fear. Mole smelled war.

They soon approached a particularly large fire near the center of the camp. Yet despite the size of the blaze, fewer shapes collected around it than had encircled any of the others. The largest man there Mole guessed to be King Cashma by his stature and by the gleam of silver on his brow.

The other two men, on either side of the king, he could not identify.

"Sire," Ashrad began, "I'm the scout you sent into the northern hills. I found these wanderers this morning. They wish to join your host."

"Do they indeed?" The King of Sharicom's voice was low-pitched and smooth. It reminded Mole of the growl of a mountain lion he had once heard on Mon Ceth. He peered through the smoke to try to catch a glimpse of the king's face across the fire. "Let them come and offer themselves, with my welcome. For on this venture we need more than a prophecy. We need swords."

Ashrad nodded and stepped back.

"I do hope they aren't outlaws, father," Mole heard one of the men whisper to the king. "Most wanderers are, you know."

A log crashed down inside the fire.

Berrian stepped forward. He seemed haggard. "I am Berrian, son of Ellarwy of Thrinedor," he said.

A storm of answer came from the other side of the fire. "The lost prince!" Cashma exclaimed, rising to his feet. "That you are not dead, as we feared, is a relief to me. It will be twice such to your father."

"I want to see him again," Berrian said, "when the battle is over."

The boy who had whispered about outlaws straightened beside Cashma. Like his father he was bronze-skinned. He wore a long yellow tunic that seemed a replica of the scout's, except for the fur-trimmed cloak and golden circlet that indicated his higher status. "If you are the lost crown prince," he said, indicating the others in the shadows with a sweep of a ringed hand, "who are your companions?"

"They are under my protection," Berrian returned, warily. "And each has proved himself in our recent ordeal in the mountains. Moleander Ammarbane, in particular—"

"Mole?" burst a vaguely familiar voice. The other prince exploded to his feet. Mole at first saw nothing but a shorter version of the first prince, but he soon recognized familiar features.

"Gareth!" he cried. He bounded over the fire. Forgetting the presence of King Cashma, he seized the boy's hand. Arien flew past Mole and embraced Gareth. Fflad, laughing, rounded the fire and began slapping Gareth on the back.

"You're alive!" Gareth shouted, looking from one to the other. "Thank the Emperor you're not dead! When news came from Thrinedor that you were missing, I almost perished with worry! I would have gone to Thrinedor to hunt for you myself if we hadn't been preparing for war. But who would have thought you'd turn up here? All of you seem a bit tired and dirty, but you're alive! I say, Mole, where'd you get that scratch on your cheek?"

"Never mind," Mole said. "Where'd you get that crown on your head?"

"Yes," Arien said. "Tell us."

Gareth beamed. "I'll tell you if you'll sit down and have something to eat. It's quite a lengthy tale."

Still crowded around Gareth, they all sat. But as soon as they found their places, Mole noticed that Berrian and Merani still hung back beyond the fire, watching stiffly. "With your leave," Mole told Gareth, "let's have Prince Berrian join us, and also Princess Merani Felleira, who has traveled with us since we left our search for Orne—"

"Orne?" Gareth searched the darkness, as if he expected to see him.

Mole briefly explained why they had left Avy-Ellarwch, what adventures they had met on the moors, and how Orne had gone into the north. "I suppose nobody could decipher my note," he finished, "so no one knew where we'd gone."

Gareth paused. "Before I tell my tale," he said, "I should introduce all of you to my father, the King of Sharicom, and my older brother, Prince Rachim." The two, looking somewhat stunned, nodded as Gareth named each of them.

"Now tell your story," Cashma commanded. "I'm anxious to see how these friends of yours—about whom I have heard so much—will take your good fortune."

"I can't believe all of you are here," Gareth said. "The letter I got from King Ellarwy is still vivid in my mind; all of you were presumed to have been killed in the Thrinefens. Ellarwy had search parties out in the fens, but they never found you."

"That's because we weren't there, at least not after a couple of days," Arien said. "Now go on with your story!"

"My father first had suspicions I was his younger son the day I arrived from Thrinedor to accept the post of loremaster. As you can see, I look a lot like Rachim; even if I didn't, my dark skin and eyes would have been enough to arouse suspicion. Nobody from Thrinedor or Pesten is so dark—I often used to wonder about my coloring myself, when I was young.

"I worked in the lore hall at Ranath Sharicom for a week before my father called me back. He brought me to the largest of the seven halls of his fortress, the Council Hall, where he and his council and Gwarthan asked me questions. The first were about lore, so I thought it was some kind of examination to check my qualifications. But the questions changed. Do you remember how Rhawn told us to remember the places where he had found us? King Cashma asked me precisely that, where I was found. I told him I'd been discovered on a knobby hill overlooking the Thrine, where fir trees grew thickly. And before I had finished answering, my father knew.

"You see, shortly after I was born, before I was even given a name, my father and mother went to Ranath Drallm to a council held by the High King. They traveled south into Crywyll and took a ship round the coasts to avoid the lands that were at the time held by the sorcerer Ammar. Then, after the council, no ships were in port, and my father, being in a hurry, decided to travel back to Sharicom by crossing Pesten with an armed guard. But goblins met them partway up the River Thrine. The goblins killed my mother. I was lost in the confusion, though my father, Rachim, and a few men escaped back to Sharicom. But the hill of the battle was exactly the same as the one I described."

"Gareth is my lost son," the king said, "without a doubt."

Mole patted Gareth on the back. "Well, Gareth, I really don't know what to say. It's not every day that one's friend becomes a prince! I'd say I'm happy for you, if it weren't such uncommonly good luck for you to find your father and become a prince both at the same time."

Arien studied Mole's expression. "I think Mole's a little jealous." She smiled at Gareth. "You know how Mole always pretended to be a king when we were little. But he's happy for you. I can tell by that light in his eyes. We're all happy for you. And for you, too, King Cashma.''

"I'm the one who ought to be happy," Gareth said. "After all, when you came out of the gloom a few minutes ago, it was almost as if you'd come back from the grave. Emperor knows, seeing you again has made a cheerful moment in a grim march—"

"Speaking of the march," Mole interrupted, "how far are we from Rathvidrian?"

At the mention of the name, faces fell. A silence swept in from the darkness, and the fire burned mutely until Cashma shifted and answered, "My army will reach Rathvidrian tomorrow." His lips drew downward. "Since all of you will be joining us, you'll be given what weapons, horses, and armor you need in the morning. But there is still time to deny your service to me," he added, "for the battlefield at Rathvidrian may claim your lives. Do any of you wish to reconsider your offers?"

Only silence answered.

"Very well, then," King Cashma said, rising. "We'll outfit you at dawn. In the meantime you may enjoy one another's company. There is meat left on the platter. Eat. Brighten these dull Downs with your laughter. And I, I must see where our wizard has gone."

The king slipped away into the blackness.

The others soon began eating, while Fflad told again what had happened on the trail from Thrinedor to Mon Cathyn. Mole hardly listened. Seated on a snow-dusted rock on the edge of the circle, his thoughts went to the chill blackness at his back. He thought he heard wingbeats above the flutter of the flames.

· 10 ·

The Voice of Rhea

THE camp woke to the horns of outriders as stallions thundered away into the hills. The valley grumbled with the hollow clank of armor and a murmur of fear, like a rising sea. Snow-bearing wind whistled over the hilltops. A dreadful cold settled in, and only a few faint beams of reddish light escaped the clouds to brighten the valley.

The moment Mole awoke, he sat up, buckled the Sword around him, and donned his doeskin cloak.

"I dreamed we were back in Thrinedor," Fflad said as he rose. Dark shapes moved everywhere in the valley; Mole watched the columns form around them while he listened to Fflad. "I was writing a poem in my room. The sun was shining in the window. Wind was stirring the tree outside, and I was thinking of the most lovely rhymes. I wish we were in Thrinedor!"

"We all want to be in Thrinedor," Berrian said quietly. "But we should be honest with ourselves. None of us may see Ranath Thrine again."

"Don't talk like that!" Arien said. "You shouldn't even *think* things like that. Look on the bright side. Today we'll defeat Ichodred. After that, we'll go back to Thrinedor and live as we did before—''

"Few tales end happily ever after, if that's what you mean," the Sword broke in. "Even if you go back to live in Thrinedor, it won't be the same. You know it. And things rarely have happy endings where evil is concerned."

Fflad clutched his cloak. "But sometimes there's joy in a sad ending," he said. "Sir Rheidol was killed by the Hardanog dragons, and yet the story is happy all the same because Rheidol accomplished what he set out to do and made the world a safer place to live."

Mole said nothing.

By the time the warriors of Sharicom were ready to march, there was enough light for them to see one another and the somber walls of the downs. But as the captains called their companies to order, a black mist swirled in; it was as if night had come again.

At every step of the horse Cashma's men had given him, Mole knew he was nearer a nightmare. He could barely make out Arien at his left and Berrian at his right; he could only see the banner of Sharicom when the staff caught some stray ray of light. The sounds around him seemed muffled and distorted, as if he heard them from across a gulf between worlds.

A cry echoed in the clouds above them; black shapes dipped from the fog, whirled, then vanished. A fearful murmur rose in the columns, and the pace slackened.

"Ride on!" King Cashma thundered. "The hawks of Fellheath cry! Soon Vivrandon will burn! We near Rathvidrian. Courage!"

The columns wound on.

At length Mole saw a long heather-covered slope rising in front of them, lifting broadly to meet the sky, and he knew, suddenly, that Rathvidrian waited beyond that hill.

Hoofbeats sounded dully in the distance; Mole saw a rider swerve down out of the gloom. Several of the king's underlords drew their swords. The footmen behind halted breathlessly. But Mole did not flinch.

The rider thundered to a halt in front of the king. "Hail, King of Sharicom!" he cried. "I am Medrin, messenger for

Daerwyn of Fellhaven; he has brought what men he can, as you wished."

"Welcome, Captain Medrin, but what is your hurry? Wasn't I to meet with Daerwyn myself?"

"Yes, my lord, but our plans have already changed. Ichodred's men found our camp and brought us to battle hours ago. We are now sore-pressed at the walls of Rathvidrian; we are wedged by a host of goblins at the ramparts and are cut off by the Fellflood in the rear. We need your help now. Or we will perish!"

Cashma called his lords around him and shouted orders, periodically demanding details of the enemy's positions from the messenger. Mole noted all that the messenger said. Soon a knot of nobles hurried down the ranks, barking orders. A contingent of riders shot away up the hill. Armor clanked, swords rattled, bowstrings twanged in test. Mole tightened the girth of his own swordbelt and gripped the reins.

"Your horses will have to go with my cavalry," King Cashma said, dismounting himself. "I don't have time to warn you of all the dangers in the coming battle. Just use your heads. Now Gareth, Moleander, Berrian, Fflad. Go with the footmen. You ladies fall back with the archers; keep out of the thick of the battle. All of you. None of you are warriors—few of you are matches for Ichodred's hawk riders, for they are shielded. We can only hope the prophecy will do its work." Mole suddenly wondered where Gwarthan was; this dependence on enchantment irked him. He very much wanted to speak with the wizard.

"This is it," Berrian said. "Look. The companies are going."

Mole dismounted. "This *is* it," he said. He faced Arien and Merani. When he looked at Arien, it suddenly was as if he and Arien were alone in a golden circle apart from the world of cold, blackness, and confusion. He saw only Arien, her glittering eyes, her oval face. "Be careful," he told her. "Don't let Merani talk you into doing anything foolish." He felt his lips twisting bitterly. "If the battle goes against us, run."

"I won't run," she said. "Not while you're in danger. Mole." She fumbled for words. "Mole, I had a dream, a dream about you. You . . . you were killed—"

Before Mole could answer, a passing captain slapped him on the back.

"Come quickly! Come now, or the battle is lost!"

A wave of warriors passed between him and Arien; he could only shout a farewell to her as he was swept away. But whether she heard him or whether she replied, he did not know.

He struggled up the icy hill, half racing the other men. Biting his lip, he drew Sodrith; the blade sparkled in the gloom. Beside him Fflad clumsily unsheathed the sword Cashma's weaponmaster had given him. Sweat beaded Mole's forehead. The wind chilled his body.

At the top of the ridge, the full force of the blast met him.

A low river valley bordered by downs on one side and rising moorland on the other lay below, lidded with clouds. Through the valley ran a broad river, the river Fellflood. Once it might have been pleasant, but now the valley stank of death. Orchards had once bordered the river, but only blackened ashes and stumps remained. In the center of the valley, sheened in smoke, waited a dark fortress in whose shadow a confusion of tiny figures swirled in battle. Horns shrilled. Weaponry crashed. Warriors poured from the hills at his side heralded by screaming trumpets; they met part of the black host at the base of the hill.

"Goblins!" Rachim cried. "Tall grey trolls and goblins. Thousands of them!"

"There are men where the hawks circle," Berrian shouted. "The hawk riders win, for the power of Rathvidrian is protecting them. But look! The goblins are falling stroke by stroke before our men. Ichodred's goblins are doomed, at least."

"But the riders," Fflad said, "they're deathless!"

"Faugh!" Mole cried. "Let's see how Ichodred's riders will stand up to the Sword!" He vaulted a boulder and charged down the hill.

Mole's voice rang, "Sodrith! Sodrith!" as he pushed into the confusion. The Sword hissed, cut, parried, struck at anything dark that barred Mole's way.

Mole soon was lost in the drunkenness of battle.

● ● ●

Arien watched with exasperation. Periodically she pushed the hair from her eyes and nocked an arrow to the string. Since she had reached her present perch on the stone ledge above the valley, she had hit nothing. The battle was such chaos she dared not loose her arrows for fear of striking one of her own men. The other archers held fire, as well, but if a goblin or troll broke free of the fray, Merani loosed a shaft. All stragglers fell under her deadly fire.

Arien's mind wandered from her work. She searched for a glimpse of any of her companions. The battle raged; it seemed as though nothing could survive in it for long. Already the lower parts of the hill were strewn with the dead. And Arien could not help but think that Fflad, Berrian, or even Mole might be among them.

Her black thoughts, however, were soon lost in activity. A fresh company of goblins fell on the Sharicom warriors at the foot of the hill. Arien, Merani, and the other archers busied themselves picking off goblins until the tide turned back toward the fortress again. Arien wished she were a better shot; she had downed only three goblins but had used half her arrows.

"Bother!" she cried. "I can't hit anything. And I've got only goblins, no riders!"

"None of us has hit a rider," Merani muttered. "It's that cursed shielding. My arrows glance off. And our warriors can't even knock them down!"

Arien felt her cheeks prickle.

Merani let another arrow fly. "I wish it were only poor archery," she grunted. "But it's magic. These Sharicom warriors fight bravely enough, but none of the hawk lords will fall. Look! We're losing the battle."

The black riders well outnumbered the men of Sharicom and their allies. More came from Rathvidrian's gate. A group of Sharicom horsemen struggled on in the center of an angry sea of battle.

Arien let the bow fall from her grip. Her hands, numbed by the wind, closed together, then rose toward her chin. The angry storm chattered in her ears, and as she watched the battle, another voice, the voice of fear, began to mutter in her mind.

All is lost, it said. Its words were cold and heavy, and

although Arien tried not to listen, the voice boomed on. They
will die, it said. All of them. Berrian is dead. Fflad is dying.
Mole will fall beneath the hooves of the Vivrandon horses. All
is lost.

Arien's quiver clattered to the ground. Her hands went to
her ears.

The voice snapped to silence.

All at once it seemed as if the sun pushed through the
clouds. The wind stopped. She was warm. The sounds of the
battle faded away to be replaced by a silence like the quiet
under summer leaves.

She smiled.

Tossing back her cloak, Arien turned to Merani. "What's
happened?" she asked, blinking back tears. "What's happened?"

But Merani didn't answer. She seemed locked into position
with an arrow half-cocked to her bow. Despair stained her
face, and her eyes were fixed on something in the valley
beneath.

Arien put a hand to her heart and looked beyond. The archers, too, stood still, like carved stone. She looked to the
valley. Half-raised spears poised, shining. Goblins, trolls, and
men alike posed, unruffled even by the wind, in combat.

Arien swallowed. Yet the situation did not seem dreamlike;
the sun, bursting from the clouds, was too bright for that.
Slowly she drew the book from her cloak and placed it
thoughtfully, reverently almost, between her palms.

The leather of the book gleamed more brightly than anything else around. The moment her fingertips touched it, she
smiled again.

Two women stood at the crest of the hill. The first wore a
gown the color of milk, whose sleeves, embroidered with
bright flowers, trailed, billowing slightly, to the ground. The
woman's arms and face were so pale they dimmed the white-
ness of her gown, but her eyes were the color of the summer
sky, and her hair foamed like a flaxen waterfall around her
shoulders. Arien felt suddenly that she had known this woman
before. But Arien knew more clearly still the flower the
woman held at her throat; it was a variety of lily she had once
seen in the south, near Aedden.

The gown of the second woman, though of an entirely different fashion, was as bright as the first. Pastel blue, it shimmered across the woman's shoulders and drifted to the earth, making the sky seem pale beside it. The woman held a spray of flowers the same color as the dress; Arien remembered having seen frozen versions of the same on Fellheath and in the Fell Downs. But the face of the second was not beautiful as was the first, though the slim, mysterious features framed in black hair were comely. Something was missing, a lack of color in the eyes. Arien frowned.

When she remembered her own clothing, Arien blushed.

But when she reached down to hide her rags, she touched silk instead of homespun. Glancing down, she saw that she was dressed in a gown of fluttering yellow, and the book she held in her fingers was no longer flamescarred.

Slowly she looked up again.

"Sisters!" she said. Then she paused to contemplate her own words. "I . . . I know you. . . . You are my sisters. Aren't you?"

"We are your sisters," said the woman in blue.

"I do know you, but I don't know from where," Arien said. Her eyes flashed in memory. "Your name is Rhea, isn't it?"

"As certainly as yours is Arien," the woman replied. She smiled, but her eyes remained stubbornly colorless. "And I am your sister, although not by blood. We are sisters because we have one mother. Amreth."

Arien chilled. "Yes, Mother Amreth," she replied, puzzled. Then more assured of herself, "Mother Amreth. Yes, I seem to know that, too. Names are coming back. But I don't know from where." Arien turned to the woman in white and exclaimed in recognition, "Cara! Is it you, Cara? I know it is! I've seen you in dreams." The woman looked at Arien but said nothing.

"Queen Cara can't answer you," Rhea said. She came to Arien. "You are mistaken about times, I think. That's why you're confused. This isn't *your time*. Not yet. You are chosen as the third, but you must remain in the world until the Last Dawn. It is so written. Cara has lived too long with Amreth to speak to you as you are now. But since I left the world only twenty years ago, I can still communicate with you."

"I don't understand. What do you mean 'since I left the world'?"

"You understand little of the works of Amreth," Rhea said, "as I did at first. We begin as mortal women, born of mortals, wed to mortals, and bound to the places of our mortal life even after we forsake the earth. Before Cara and I were chosen, we were like you. Cara lived near Aedden, where she and her husband, King Llarandil, reigned over the Kingdoms for many years. I am Rhea, Lady Fellflood, wife of Fifran II, and once Queen of Vivrandon."

"But now you are an enchantress," Arien said, glancing back at the grey stillness of Merani and the battle beyond. "And your enchantment brought me here."

"Yes. I'm not as powerful as I once was, for now you have been chosen, and the enchantment of Amreth is always strongest in the youngest daughter, for it becomes unused in the older." Rhea nodded toward Cara. "Cara hasn't used her powers since the Battle of Northmarch."

"Battle," Arien repeated, somewhat blankly. She swung around to face the valley. "Yes. The battle. All this almost made me forget." She thought of Mole. "We're losing the battle, Rhea; the men of Vivrandon are deathless. If you were once Queen of Vivrandon, you must know that. Please, if you are as powerful as you seem, do something!"

Rhea's eyes fell.

"I know you may feel loyalty to Vivrandon," Arien went on hastily, "but so does Merani, and she's helping. I know you're not evil. I can tell. And I know you're powerful. You can help us! Look! Men are dying! Sharicom is almost defeated. For all I know, my friends may be bleeding to death down there. I'm sure there's something you can do. You must know some spell that will turn the tide!"

Rhea's eyes remained dull. "I can't help you."

Arien put her hands to her hips. "Why not?"

Rhea shifted. She looked up but could not meet Arien's glare. "Because," she said at last, "I'm the one causing Vivrandon to win."

Arien shuddered, as if a cold draft had reached her. Looking to Cara's face for explanation, Arien saw Cara's eyes go dim. A cloud moved over the sun. With the darkness came a dread verse to Arien's memory.

> One shall fell enchantment find
> The gates of Vivrandon to bind.

"You're not . . . *evil*?" Arien stammered. "You're not on Ichodred's side?"

"Oh no! Amreth's daughters can't be evil. They can only be foolish!"

"Well, if you aren't evil, why are you shielding the lives of the hawk lords? Do you realize how many good men they've killed?"

"Yes!" Rhea's answer was almost a sob. "I know. I know all too well. But I didn't mean for it to happen. It worked at first, before Ichodred. Try to understand! The enchantment of Amreth is the strongest on earth; oaths sworn by Amreth are unbreakable. Years ago, after my husband Fifran died, I began to grow closer to Amreth and discover my powers. By that time, my son, Ichodron, had been king five years; I grew tired of life and wished to have my time and go with Amreth. But I loved my son and Vivrandon, too, and I wished to leave them a lasting gift. Just before my time, my power was at its peak. Hoping to insure the strength of my country, I cast a spell on the royal warriors of Vivrandon so that no weapon could harm them in battle. And foolishly I oathed for the protection always to remain in Vivrandon; I promised never to lift the spell. Then I left, thinking I had done my part for good. Little did I realize the evil that would come of it!"

"I understand," Arien said softly. "That's why only the hawk riders are protected then. Merani said that a greater power than Ichodred watched over Vivrandon. She was right. But couldn't you ask Gwarthan to remove the spell? He's here, you know. Otherwise Ichodred will win the battle; after this he will march on Sharicom and Pesten and Thrinedor, and no one will be able to stop him!"

Rhea frowned. "No power is stronger than Amreth's magic. Not the power of wizards. Not the sorcery of necromancers. Nothing but Amreth's magic can undo Amreth's magic."

"Then let Cara destroy your spell!"

"Haven't you listened? Amreth's magic is with her newest daughter. Cara is powerless. I might be, too, if it hadn't been for my oath. Haven't you guessed why you're here?" Rhea extended an arm toward Arien. "*You* shall break the enchantment!"

"Me?" Arien stammered. "How?"

"You are the third," Rhea said simply. "The power is in you; it is swelling even now. When it comes to a crest, you must use it."

"But I don't know how!"

Rhea looked at her beseechingly. "You must discover the sources of your own power, Arien. I can't help you."

The bright world swam before Arien's eyes. Rhea's face darkened, nearly disappearing into shadow. Arien flung out her hands, wrinkled her forehead with worry, but she could see no answer to Rhea's riddle.

Then her eyes met Cara's. And she saw part of the answer there, as she had often seen a new twist to a familiar tree trunk from its reflection on a still summer pond. Ideas and actions began to take on new patterns, and mysteries of the past fell into place.

> But Fellflood's angry oath shall break
> For a wilted blossom's sake.

Arien lifted the book, opened it, and fumbled in its pages. Her fingers curled around the dried flower she had carried there from Thrinedor. She drew it out and held it up. At once she could feel it becoming moist and smooth again.

"Excellent, Arien," Rhea said. "Now, break my foolish spell."

What happened next was hard for Arien to understand, and afterward when she contemplated the experience, only a few impressions reappeared.

First she could no longer see. Not in the ordinary sense. Instead she *felt*. She sensed living evil, but she was no longer afraid of it. Like fireflies around a torch, lesser presences danced and shifted around her, occasionally shimmering like shards of glass or sinking into a swirling sea of ideas. Then she began to grow. First she was bigger than a hill, then bigger than the high downs; then she towered over mountains, rivers, kingdoms, whole worlds. And they were all the same to her. Her fingers became lightning, her voice thunder. Nothing mattered beyond herself. Yet she noticed small things, a particularly perfect flake of snow falling in the Far North and blue moonlight on a butterfly's wing in the Land Beyond Dawn. But her attention was focused below her. When she sensed the agony of men, wrath stormed within her. Gripping the flower, she roared:

"Spell, be broken!"

The earth shook. Lightning struck at her feet. She felt the evil presence sputter away like a torch thrust into a river. Then she sank, shrank, withered, crumpled into herself like papers in a bonfire until she found herself face to face with Rhea.

Rhea's eyes were now storm blue.

"It's done," she said. "Now, go on your way, Arien. Your power will soon diminish, just as a great tide must ebb; but when your power begins to rise again, you will know that your time to leave the world approaches."

Looking down, Arien found herself dressed again in her threadbare travel clothes. "Let me stay," she pleaded, "just a little longer." A hollowness engulfed her.

"Parting is hard, but you must go."

"Please!"

The brilliant gowns faded. Rhea and Cara became translucent, then transparent. "Farewell," came the voice of Rhea, muted, removed. "Farewell, until your time comes."

The world darkened, and the Daughters of Amreth melted away.

• 11 •

The Dark Between

"ARIEN! Arien! Wake up!"

A spark kindled in the back of Arien's mind, and she forced herself out of unconsciousness. She felt the wind screaming across her cheeks and knotting her hair. Opening her eyes, she saw a shadow looming over her. Beyond were sullen clouds threaded through with black smoke. There was a dim snap of flames far off and nearer the quick breaths of Merani Felleira, who stooped over her.

Merani's cheeks were more ruddy than Arien had ever seen them, but her hands were white. "Are you all right? I looked back to get another arrow from my quiver, and when I looked forward again, you had dropped your bow. You fell to the ground. Are you hurt?"

"No. I don't think so," Arien murmured, pressing her eyes closed in order to remember beyond her meeting with Rhea. "I think I fainted."

"Well, you might have been dead and I couldn't have done anything for you," Merani said. "As soon as you dropped, a band of goblins started to storm our position. I've been loosing arrows for half an hour straight!"

Arien pushed herself up and brushed the hair from her eyes.

150

"I'd better get my bow before the next attack comes, then."

Merani laughed. "The next attack? There won't be another one. The battle's over. Yes, it's over," she repeated, as if to assure herself. "While you fainted, the tide began to turn; the goblins that just attacked were the last in the valley. And they're all dead now."

"What about the others? Have you seen Mole?"

Merani helped Arien to her feet. "I haven't. But the battle ended only a few moments ago. I haven't exactly been looking. I had to see about you first."

"I suppose," Arien said. She squinted into the valley as she brushed the snow from her legs. Vapor still rose from the river, and a pall of sooty smoke closed over most of the battlefield. Arien saw scattered men standing, grouped into clusters, or bending over the bodies of the many fallen, which made the valley a grisly spectacle. The sun sending shafts of red light through the clouds revealed patches of smoldering fire and pooling blood. The wind, rising off the river, carried to the hills the stench of burning and the groans of the dying.

When Arien's eyes at last pierced the shroud of smoke surrounding the fortress, she saw that most of the living had gathered at the gate. Companies of men brought together two banners, the first that of Fellhaven, the second that of Sharicom. They were thrust in the earth together.

"They just finished off the last hawk rider by the gate," Merani said, frowning at the scene. "By the shouts I heard, I'd say they slew Ichodred as well." Her lips hardened. "I hope they did. If they didn't, if he escaped, I'll track him down myself."

"Never mind Ichodred. I doubt he got away by the look of things. But what about Berrian? And Fflad? And Mole? I don't see them."

"They're at the gate, most likely. Don't worry. They'll come back to us soon." But in spite of her words, Merani scanned the haze anxiously. "See!" she shouted in a moment. "I told you. I think that's Fflad who's coming up the hill now."

"I'm not so sure," Arien returned. "It doesn't look like him."

But it was Fflad, though Arien could scarcely recognize

him. His hair was matted with sweat, his face drawn with pain, and his arm red with blood. An empty scabbard banged against his knee. Only his eyes, bright with excitement, resembled his former self.

Arien ran to him and caught his hand, touched his chin. "How badly are you hurt?" She examined the cuts on his face.

"Hurt?" Fflad said vaguely. "Eh . . . I don't think I'm hurt at all. Just banged up a little."

"Good! I mean, it's good you're not too wounded—Merani, do you have a clean bit of cloth on you for this cut—the battle seemed so fierce." She looked Fflad in the eyes. "Have you seen Mole?"

Fflad winced as Arien pried at the cut on his arm. "Mole. Hm. I haven't seen him recently. But if you're worried about Berrian, I saw *him* a few minutes ago, catching a word with King Cashma by the gate. He doesn't have a scratch on him, that prince. His hair isn't even ruffled!"

"I wasn't worried about Berrian," Arien said, dabbing at the runs of blood on Fflad's forearm with the bit of gauze Merani handed to her. "Berrian has sense. But Mole doesn't. You know how he is. Ever since he found that Sword in Mon Ceth, he's felt he has to use it!" She folded the cloth double and started her work anew. "This time I have a feeling, don't ask me why, that something awful's happened to him."

"What? To Mole?" Fflad laughed, but he closed a hand over his mouth when he saw Arien's face. "I know what you mean about Mole. He sometimes doesn't know when to stop—"

"How long has it been since you've seen him?" Merani broke in.

"I was too busy dodging swords and arrows most of the time to notice," Fflad reflected. "But I saw him just after the battle started. He was cutting down goblins like a whirlwind. I saw him meet some hawk riders. But he couldn't kill them, not even with the Sword—"

"Did you see what happened to him after that?"

"The flash happened after that. You remember the flash. You must have seen it, even up here. I thought it was lightning when I saw it, but a few minutes later someone told me it was magic. It must have been magic, for I saw Mole kill a Vivrandon warrior only a moment after it happened. Gwarthan must have broken the spell. Or the prophecy broke it. One or the other.''

"Magic be blasted," Arien snapped. "What about Mole?"

Fflad looked into space. But then his face brightened. "Oh yes," he said as Arien followed a bruise on his throat with her finger. "We started winning after that, thanks to whoever broke the spell. King Cashma's cavalry began riding down the hawk riders. We footmen closed in on the gate, where the hawk lords, all in black, protected Prince Ichodred. I remember seeing the scoundrel go down; one of his own men turned on him."

"As he deserved," Merani said, tight-lipped.

"Afterwards, someone tried to get to Ichodred's body, but he met a huge man in a black cape who didn't fall even when run through with a sword. It must have been that sorcerer, the Black Counselor of Vivrandon. He must have protected his life as Ammar did, for it seemed nothing could kill him. That was when Mole came. He had quite a bout with the sorcerer. It was awful to see; the rest of us pulled back. The sorcerer must have thrown a dozen spells at Mole to keep him off; the rest of us heard thunder and saw flashes of fire. But Mole didn't give up. He lunged and drove the Sword right into the Black Counselor's throat. But the worst part was when the Black Counselor died. He didn't die quickly, as Ammar did. He shouted at Mole and threw shafts of lightning at him and cursed him."

"Cursed him?" Arien's fingers, straightening Fflad's collar, froze. "How?"

Fflad coughed. His eyes widened. "I'd rather not say."

"Tell me," Arien demanded. "Now."

Fflad swallowed. "He condemned Mole to die before the sun set."

Arien suddenly became aware of the low slant of the sun's rays over her shoulder.

Merani tipped her head back to the sky. "I see Cwyller coming this way," she said. "I'll send him to look for Mole."

"I don't need your hawk," Arien shot back. She slapped the bloodsoaked bit of cloth into Fflad's hand. "I'm going to look for Mole myself!" But Fflad stopped her.

"Wait. The battlefield is no place for you right now. Look! Here comes Berrian. He'll know about Mole. And there's someone with him!"

"It isn't Mole," Arien countered. "It's Gareth."

"But one of them is sure to know where Mole is."

"Look!" Merani gasped. "They're carrying something between them."

Berrian and Gareth were approaching over the rocky ground at a jolting pace. And they did indeed carry something, a sort of bier, between them.

"Where's Mole?"

Closing his eyes, Berrian laid his burden down and stepped aside. The others did not move as Arien approached, holding one hand near her cheek, hardly daring to look but unable not to.

Dull and bloodstained, the gems of Sodrith glimmered in the grip of a waxen hand. Mole's eyes and lips were mere bloodless lines on his face; tangled hair clumped with blood fell back to reveal a pattern of empty cuts and colorless bruises. The right side of his tunic ran with blood that fell, a deadly crimson rain, onto the stones.

"Arien." Fflad moved behind her. He glanced at Mole, then held out a shaky hand to her.

She stared dumbly at Mole. "No, Fflad," she said. "No." She fell to her knees beside Mole, touched his cheek, then drew back her hand as if it were hot. Then her hands went to the Sword, which in a moment of fury she tried to pry away. But his locked fingers did not yield.

She lifted her head. "Berrian. Where was he?"

"By the gate," he croaked, "as you see him now. When Gareth and I found him, he was breathing. We tried to get help—but there were so many wounded and so few healers. Our only choice was to try to find someone; we decided to bring him here. He spoke to us when we lifted him to the stretcher. But he's been silent since—"

Arien held her fingers above his lips. But she could feel no breath. "He spoke," she said in a voice pinched high. "Tell me what he said."

Beneath the skin, Berrian's jaw tightened.

"Tell me!"

Gareth stepped forward. "He told us not to let you see him, Arien. But he told us to tell you . . . to tell you . . ." his eyes flickered, ". . . that he loved you."

Arien laid a hand on Mole's cheek; it was almost as cold as the rocks at her knees, but it was strangely softer. Quickly she tore strips from her robe and began to push back Mole's hair and wipe the blood from his face. She could not help but notice how well-cut Mole's features were, even when marred and cursed by death.

"He died well?" Her words were not really a question.

Fflad squatted beside her. "Would Mole die any other way?" he replied. "Can't you see it on his face? He died nobly. He died a prince." Fflad sniffed. "And, considering it all, it really isn't sad. Was it sad when Sir Rheidol died after he had killed the dragons? No. His death was noble, so the tale ends happily. Not with sadness."

"But this isn't a tale!" Arien said. She wanted to say more, but the words thickened in her throat. She tried to sponge the blood from Mole's side but found she could not, for there was too much of it.

The wind came up. It grew colder.

Then Arien saw the ash staff resting on Mole's far side. She leaned over him and snatched it, but in the process something fell from her cloak and rang faintly against the smudged iron of the Sword.

Arien hooked the staff in her arm, then straightened.

The wind opened the pages of her book, where it had fallen, to reveal the pressed flower. Hardly daring to breathe, Arien checked to see whether any of the others were watching before bringing the arien to her body.

"By all the powers dying within me," she whispered, "let Mole live again!"

She was swept at once into a vivid vision of darkness.

"He has died," said an expressionless voice. "He walks the final corridor. He has already seen the happiness beyond. He won't come back. Once he steps over the bright threshold, he will be lost to you forever."

"By the powers of Amreth," she heard herself cry, "I call him back."

"Amreth's enchantment can call back the dead," the voice replied, "but only if the dead wish to come back. He is nearly there—"

"Mole!" Arien shouted. Her voice echoed, as if she were in a great catacomb. "Mole! It's Arien! Come back!"

"Oh, don't bother me now, Ari," Mole's voice buzzed, sounding distant in the darkness. "I don't want to come back. Dying isn't easy, you know. I don't want to have to go through it all again. Besides, I can see Llan and Rhawn just up ahead. Let me go!"

"I won't let you go," Arien shouted fiercely. "I won't. You can't go. You can't! By the Emperor, come back!"

His voice was thinner. "I'm sorry, Arien."

"Sorry!" Arien burst. She felt her power dwindling, her hold on Mole waning. "Mole! Must I talk sense into you even when you're dead?" Suddenly she felt the ash staff, still tucked under her arm. "I have the staff here, Mole. Do you remember what it's for?"

"Yes," came the faint answer. "But—"

"Nothing has changed. Nothing! You're still supposed to take care of us. We need you." She paused. "*I* need you. Please."

There was a long pause.

"All right." Mole's voice sighed. "I'll return. But I won't like coming back into winter. It's so warm here!"

Coughing.

The blackness swirled away.

Coughing. As soon as Arien opened her eyes, the wind seized the fragile flower. Yet Arien didn't watch it go, for Mole's head lifted from his bier, and he burst into a fit of coughing.

"He's alive!" she screamed. "He's alive!"

The others rushed to gather around. "He is!" Berrian shouted. Berrian drew the cloak from his shoulder, wadded it, and wedged it under Mole's arm.

"It's a miracle," Fflad squealed. "I thought for certain he was dead."

Arien looked up. "Someone get a healer. Quickly!"

"I'll go!" Berrian said. "They'll give a healer to a prince."

"I'll go, too," Merani said. "They'll listen to a girl, even if they won't listen to a prince."

While the others dashed away, Fflad and Gareth pressed in. Mole breathed more evenly now; yet his chest rose and fell gustily, and Arien held Berrian's cloak tightly to his side to combat renewed bleeding. But she could not help but smile at the uncomprehending twitchings of his cheeks as his eyes opened.

Troubled, his eyes searched the sky, then focused on Arien.

"Arien," he mumbled, "did we win?"

Arien smiled and worked the Sword from his hand. "We won," she said.

· 12 ·

Falconflight

BY twilight of the fifth day after the battle, Mole had recovered enough strength to walk. So when Berrian and Arien decided to go to the top of the hill nearest the camp, Mole, eager to try out his legs again, insisted on going with them. And at the last moment Gwarthan appeared, free from his duties and able to go along. So Fflad, Merani, and Gareth decided to go as well.

Daylight drained away as they climbed the rough hill toward a linden grove. Glancing behind him as they went, Mole saw the whole west afire in red, but belts of greyish cloud still hovered over the ruins of Rathvidrian. An evening wind brushed across the River Fellflood; its waters sparkled like the scales of a fire serpent. The same wind ruffled the grey walls of the tents, though soon, Mole reflected, those would be gone.

As they walked, Fflad moved in between Mole and Gwarthan, holding the hoop he had found in the outlaws' backpack. It glittered in the low slant of the sun as he handed it to Gwarthan.

"I've wanted to ask you about this for a long time," Fflad said. "It seems magical." While Fflad explained where they had found the circlet, Gwarthan turned it in his hands.

"I've seen nothing like it before," he said presently. "But it does seem to be an instrument of magic. It may have been used by one of the seven wizards who lived in the Fell Downs before Vivrandon became a kingdom. The outlaws could have stolen it from a barrow or a trove."

"But what is it? What's it for?"

"I don't know. But I dare say you'll find out sooner or later, at a time you least expect. Keep it safe in the meantime. And don't do anything foolish like put it on your head under a full moon."

Fflad nodded and slipped the hoop into his coat.

The seven spread themselves beneath some lindens, on the soft mesh of dead leaves and grass. Cwyller sailed away from Merani and alighted, henlike, on a high branch. Fflad and Gareth found a boulder to share. Berrian sprawled back against the trunk of a tree and buried his hands in the leaves. Mole, winded a little from the ascent, laid himself out on the hillside so he could watch the play of light and shadow across the battlefield. The Sword's belt bruised his hips, so he unbuckled it and handed it to Arien, who coupled the Sword and staff in her hands and laid them on her lap.

Gwarthan, however, remained on his feet. Tugging at his beard, he watched the sun tuck itself beneath the horizon. Mole wondered what he was thinking, what knowledge of new sorcerers or new wars the enchanter had as he peered out over the darkening heaths.

Quiet reigned until the first star appeared. Mole could not help but notice it was Orygath, the pole star.

"Gwarthan," Arien said, "after all that's happened"— she glanced at Mole—"after all that's changed, what will happen now?"

The wizard turned his head. "To Vivrandon? I suspect the High King will choose Daerwyn of Fellhaven to rule. The land has suffered much, but it will be quieter in years to come. In time its people will flourish again, and the ruts and scars of this valley will disappear under crops and houses and years. But don't think that you've seen the last battle of your lives. I guarantee you'll each see many more. Not all of them will be fought with swords, either. But each must be fought, for even though Evil is constantly defeated, it rises again. It will always rise again. It is rising, even now!''

One of Mole's wounds smarted. When he twitched, Arien's hand went to his shoulder. "Yes, but I wish you wouldn't mention it," she said. "Not right now. I don't want to think about it. Besides, that isn't what I meant to ask. I mean, what's to happen with *us*?"

"What do you want to happen to you?" Gwarthan returned.

"I'll go back to Ranath Sharicom," Gareth said. His eyes were on his father's tent. "Ranath Sharicom is a very large castle, though. It sometimes feels empty. Any of you who like can come back to Sharicom and live with me."

"No offense to you, Gareth, but I don't think I'd like Sharicom," Fflad said. "I don't like mutton, and besides, I want to go back to Avy-Ellarwch. I was in the middle of writing two poems when we went after Orne, and I'm dying to finish them!"

"I want to return to Thrinedor, too," Berrian said from beneath the trees. "But you know, as silly as this may sound, I don't want to *stay* at Ranath Thrine for very long after we get there. I might remember I'm crown prince if we stay too long. I might fall back into some bad habits."

"I could stand no more than a couple of weeks at Avy-Ellarwch myself," Mole said. "Not that there's anything wrong with the place, it's just that I need something new."

"But if we don't go to Sharicom and if we don't stay in Thrinedor," Arien reasoned, "where will we go? I hope you don't have in mind another adventure. I'm really not up to it."

"Neither am I." Mole sighed. "I was thinking of something just as exciting, but somewhat more tame. I'd like to go to Ranath Drallm."

"The seat of the High King?" Gwarthan asked. He looked at Mole keenly. "Good! Moleander, you don't know how happy you've made me by saying that. You see, I'm bound for Drallm myself, to give the High King a report of what's happened here. I was thinking—that's why I came to your tent—that you might like to travel there with me. But I kept quiet until you mentioned it."

"But Ranath Drallm is far," Arien objected.

"And what would we do when we got there?" Fflad asked.

"I'm sure that High King Gion will take you all under his protection. Especially when I tell him what you've all done here." Gwarthan glanced at Arien. "Fflad, you could become the greatest minstrel in the Kingdoms by studying in the libraries of Drallm. Arien, as lovely as you are, you could marry the most handsome lord of the coast kingdoms!" Mole reddened until Gwarthan turned and added, with a twinkle in his eye, "And you, Moleander, could become a captain of the High King's armies. If you use that Sword of yours with intelligence, you might even become Gion's High Captain."

"I would be content to be a stable boy if I could serve the High King," Mole replied. "Then it's settled. We're to go to Ranath Drallm. By way of Thrinedor, of course."

"Do you suppose," Berrian said after a pause, "that I could come along as well, at least for a visit? I've never seen Ranath Drallm nor met the High King. I'd speak to my father about leaving this time, of course. But I want to go." He nudged Mole with his boot. "Besides, someone has to go along to keep Mole out of trouble."

"The High King would be delighted to have you, Prince Berrian."

A husky voice spoke from a white blur in the darkness. "Now that Ichodred's dead, I'd just as soon leave Vivrandon as stay," Merani said. "And I'll bet that High King Gion could use a fine hawk like Cwyller in breeding. And he might need another archer—"

"He might get a lovely lady in the bargain," Gwarthan said. "And I don't think the others would go anywhere without you, Merani."

Merani didn't answer. But later Mole thought he heard her crying.

"Now then," Gwarthan said crisply, "if we all agree, we'll start for Ranath Thrine in the morning. We can't forget it's still winter, and we ought to make sure we're off Fellheath before the next blizzard!"

Then, at last, Gwarthan sat down. Mole saw his silhouette drop away from the blazing swirls of stars. And he began to imagine the southern stars, swimming over the rising rim of the sea. He began to imagine the smell of seaweed and the sound of the breakers on the sand. He had almost lulled himself to sleep when Arien shook his shoulder.

"Mole," she said urgently. "Mole!"

"What is it? Ouch—watch your hands—you hit my face that time."

"I'm sorry. But it's your Sword. Something's wrong! Something's changed, and I don't know why I didn't see it before. Do you remember how one of the three rubies on the hilt turned into a sapphire after you killed Ammar at Ranath Caeodd? Another one's turned; only the biggest ruby's left."

Mole twisted around. "How can you tell?" he asked skeptically. "I mean, it's dark. I can't even see where the Sword is." Mole let his head relax into Arien's lap. "Besides," he said, "a ruby can't turn into a sapphire just like that. It's impossible."

"It did before!"

"Well, even so, I think it's all nonsense. I always hear about enchantment and that sort of thing, but I never get to see any of it. You know, I'm beginning to think there isn't any magic besides the kind the black sorcerers use!"

Arien smiled. "Perhaps." He heard her lift the Sword from her lap and place it in the leaves beside him. "Maybe, Moleander Ammarbane, you're right."

Her laughter glittered like the sparkle of stars on the river.

Dear Fantasy Reader,
Ace Books has brought you the best
in adult fantasy for over thirty years.
Now we are pleased to offer the very
best in young adult fantasy, under
our MagicQuest logo. MagicQuest
brings classic and popular works of
YA fantasy into paperback for fantasy
readers and collectors of all ages.

___ 80839-5/$2.25 **THE THROME OF THE ERRIL OF SHERILL**
Patricia A. McKillip

The Throme of Erril of Sherill, a book of songs more beautiful than
the stars themselves does not exist. But if the Cnite Caerles is to
win the sad-eyed daughter of the King of Everywhere, he must find
it, and so he sets out on an impossible quest...
Illustrated by Judith Mitchell. By the World Fantasy Award-winning
author of *The Forgotten Beasts of Eld* and *The Riddle-Master Trilogy*.

___ 65956-X/$2.25 **THE PERILOUS GARD**, *Elizabeth Marie Pope*

Based loosely on the ballad *Tam Lin*, this is the tale of a young man
in bondage to the Queen of the Fairies, and a young woman who
ventures deep into the fairy realms to win him back again...
Newberry Honor Winner and ALA Notable Book.

___ 03115-3/$2.25 **THE ASH STAFF**, *Paul R. Fisher*

Mole is the oldest of six orphans raised by an old sorcerer in the
magical land of Mon Ceth. When their protector dies, Mole must take
up his staff and become the leader of the orphan band. As they leave
the safety of their mountain, little do they know that the are about
to plunge headlong into war. First in the popular *Ash Staff* series.

___ 82630-X/$2.25 **TULKU**, *Peter Dickinson*

Peter Dickinson is best known to fantasy readers for *The Blue Hawk* — and for *Tulku,* a splendid tale of a young American boy in 19th century China who travels to the myth-ridden mountains of Tibet — where the magic is real. An ALA Notable Book.

___ 16621-0/$2.25 **THE DRAGON HOARD**, *Tanith Lee*

Lee has been called "The Princess of Royal Heroic Fantasy" by *The Village Voice* — but before she became a bestselling adult writer Ms. Lee had already made a name for herself with several tales of YA fantasy adventure. Wacky, wonderful and thoroughly magical, Ms. Lee's YA fiction is available in paperback for the first time.

Prices may be slightly higher in Canada.